Isle of Galkirk

Witten by

Louis J. Webber.

Edited by Charlotte Demedts.

Artwork by Giles Demedts.

First Printed in Great Britain by
Obex Publishing Ltd in 2021

1 2 4 6 8 10 9 7 5 3

Paperback ISBN: 978-1-913454-42-5
Hardback ISBN: 978-1-913454-43-2
eBook ISBN: 978-1-913454-44-9

A CIP catalogue record for this book is available
from the British Library

Obex Publishing Limited
Reg. No. **12169917**

For Grandad Pete, Grandad Fred,

Mr. Reck, and Florian Schneider.

Table of Contents

Prologue.

11/02/83

Mr. Johnston,

Firstly, on behalf of everyone here at Mumma's Own Breakfast Co., congratulations on winning the 'Mamma's Name Game' competition.

As you're well aware, by winning the competition, we'll be sending you for a weekend trip (including travel, accommodation, and £100 spending money) to a UK destination of your choice.

However, there has been an issue with your request.

Sadly, we must reiterate for the third time that Galkirk Island is a fictional place. Therefore, we regret to inform you that we cannot accept this as the location of your choice. If you cannot provide us with an adequate location within the next two weeks, we will have no choice but to withdraw you from the competition, meaning you'll no longer be entitled to our grand prize.

Please find enclosed one last request form. As before, please fill in this form and send it back to us. Should we receive this with an adequate location before the end of March, we will begin to process the application.

Thank you for your co-operation, and your continued loyalty to Mamma's Own Breakfast Co.

We understand you have many options when it comes to your first meal of the day, and we're extremely proud to announce that our customers have voted us the number 1 cereal brand in the UK for the 4th year running.

Many thanks,
Thomas J. Walter
Community Manager

Chapter 1:
Welcome.

Harold woke to the sound of banging on the cabin window. Over and over. As he began to rub his eyes, he winced. Less than a week had passed, so it was no surprise that the left side of his face was still hurting, especially around the eye. Using the back of his hand, he felt where the swelling had been. It was no longer warm to the touch, but it was still tender. Catching a glimpse of himself in the window, he could see that his eye was still dark around the outside. It wasn't the best look for a first impression, but if there was anywhere he could go where he wouldn't be judged on how he looked, it was here.

The banging on the window continued. As Harold unbolted the cabin door, the wind blew it open with a crash. The rain was falling like stair rods, and with a hand sheltering his eyes, Harold looked for the captain. The captain hadn't noticed that Harold was no longer in the cabin and continued to bang on the window with a closed fist. The boat began to rock violently from side to side, throwing Harold into the side of the cabin. He tried to steady himself, grabbing hold of whatever he could to keep himself upright.

After a few minutes of trying to keep his stomach content where it should be, the rocking stopped. The sea became calm and the boat steadied out to a smooth, light sway. The thick fog prevented Harold from seeing what was ahead, but he wondered what the captain could see, since he was preparing a thick rope as if they'd arrived. Harold grabbed his suitcase and made his way towards the captain. "Are we here? I can't see anyth-"

"100 quid," interrupted the captain, "and I'm not taking your case. This is as far as I go."

"Of course." said Harold. As he handed over a handful of £20 notes, he could make out a small dock ahead of them. The captain threw the rope toward the dock with one hand, whilst stuffing the notes into his pocket with the other. As he tightened the rope, Harold could see a narrow, cobblestone path leading up past the dock.

"Before you go, I need to give you something." said the captain. He headed into the cabin and slowed the boat to a crawl. When he emerged, he had a small package and a stack of letters bundled together. "Give this to the Czar, will you?" Harold raised an eyebrow, assuming it was some kind of joke. But as the captain looked back into Harold's eyes, he could see the captain was being sincere. Harold took the package under his arm and slipped the letters into his inside pocket. "Thank you. I'd best be off." The boat was barely at the dock, but the captain had already made his way back into the cabin. With a leap, Harold made it off the boat and onto the damp, wooden dock. As he turned to face the boat, it's engines roared as it started to turn, and within seconds the boat was barely visible through the fog. Harold turned towards the cobblestone path. The rain had eased into a drizzle that felt constant in the air, making his hair stick to his forehead. Brushing his hair back, Harold exhaled deeply. He'd made it.

Making his way up the cobblestone path, Harold could make out what looked like two large, stone houses, with the path passing between them. He couldn't see any lights or signs of life as he got closer, which wasn't surprising considering it was the early hours.

The space between the buildings was narrow, as if the path were built after the houses, and rain was sliding down the stone walls, with the moonlight making it look as though they were moving.

As he reached the end of the ally, he stood in what seemed like a town square. There was no sign of life in any of the several buildings that faced the centre, where a decorative fountain sat. Everywhere looked clean. Deserted, but clean. On the far side was what looked like a town hall built of dark red bricks, which seemed to fit the instruction he'd been given. Soaked through to his skin, he made his way past the fountain to the heavy wooden doors of the red building. Careful not to wake anyone inside, he pulled the door open by the old-fashioned handle and let himself in. He twisted the door handle as he closed it behind him, making sure not to cause a scene.

Inside the building were several round tables accompanied by chairs, and a bar at one end with stairs behind it. It wasn't what Harold was expecting, but it was somewhat comforting to see what looked like a pub in a place like this. He placed his suitcase on the table and took a seat. It wasn't until now that Harold realised how tired he was, and how much his face still hurt. He pushed his seat back and rested his head against the wall, listening to the rain pick up again outside. As he closed his eyes, he wondered if he should find where his room might be, or spend the night where he was. After all, at least he was inside now. And, most importantly, he was safe.

As he began to drift off, the doors beside him burst open, startling Harold. In walked a man in a green, crushed velvet suit, his hair brushed back behind his ears. He didn't seem wet at all and was wearing two rings on his right hand. He turned to face Harold and looked him up and down.

"Mr. Kobbs," said the man, "you made it, finally. Some of the residents said they saw you arriving. No raincoat? You must be cold. I'll fix you a drink." The man held Harold by the shoulders and embraced him. "Let me guess, you're a whisky man? All you Scots are." The stranger made his way over to the bar, while Harold just stood there watching him.

"Sorry," said Harold, still in shock, "...you are?" The man looked Harold in the eyes once again. He was confident and overly flamboyant – not the type of person Harold expected to encounter in a place like this.

"I'm the man. The big cheese. Numero Uno. But most importantly, Mr. Kobbs, I'm your salvation."

"Oh. Well, I'm looking for Christian Wile? You see, she and I have been writing to each other an-"

"Christian Wile?" said the stranger, "Oh, *that* Christian Wile. Well, you've found her." The stranger turned to face Harold and smiled. His eyes were a pale blue and his nose came to a sharp point like a caricature.

"You're Christian Wile? Sorry," Harold said with his hand shielding his eyes "I was expecting-"

"Someone different? A lady, perhaps? It's fine, I should really stop signing off my letters with a kiss. It often gives people the wrong impression. But, not that there's anything wrong with a man who signs off his letters with a kiss." Christian brought two glasses of whisky over to the table and took a seat, gesturing for Harold to do the same. "But I do hope that's not why you've come here, Mr. Kobbs. After all, I'm not sure Maria would appreciate that." He took a sip of his drink, refusing to break eye contact whilst he drank.

"No. No, that's not why I'm here. Sorry, Mrs- Mr. Wile. I'm very tired. Do you think maybe you can tell me where my room is? And please, call me Harold." Christian looked down at his drink. His smiling, cheery demeanor suddenly changed to a very stern, serious look.

"There are a few rules you'll need to know before you can call yourself a resident, Harry. But the main ones are these; you don't ask questions. You're thankful for each day. And, most importantly, the past is the past." Christian downed the rest of his drink and rose to his feet. "Tomorrow is market day. Introduce yourself to the residents, get to know people, and for god's sake, try the chicken rolls Mrs. Sands makes. If it's not the new start that people come here for, it's those chicken rolls. Exotic? No. But tasty? Like you wouldn't believe."

Christian was a slim man, with legs that looked like drainpipes in trousers. He made his way towards the wooden door as Harold remembered the packages from the captain.

"Oh. Mr. Wile, I've got these for 'The Czar'? They're from the boat captain." Harold held out the parcel with one hand, whilst reaching for the letters with the other.

"Is there a small, brown envelope? Possibly not sealed?" As Harold looked through the envelopes, he saw it. Unmarked and unsealed, nestled in between the others. He handed it to Christian, who was waiting with an outstretched hand. Christian opened it, revealing a handful of £20 notes inside. He counted them out loud until he reached £100. "Perfect. Thank you, Mr. Kobbs." He put the money back into the envelope and picked up the rest of the items from the captain. "Up the stairs, second room on the left is yours. You should find everything in there you sent ahead, as well as everything you'll need to make yourself comfortable."

"Thank you, Mr. Wile. Will I see you at the market tomorrow?" Christian turned to face Harold once more, with the cheery demeanor back in his eyes.

"Oh yes, Mr. Kobbs. You'll see me there, with a chicken roll in hand no doubt." As he opened the door to the outside, he glanced over his shoulder. "Enjoy your stay here, Mr. Kobbs. But remember, the only baggage you bring here is physical. The past has already happened. Here on the Isle of Galkirk," He turned to face Harold, "we all start fresh."

Chapter 2:
Begin.

The smell of cooked meat filled the small space that was now Harold's home. With only a single bed and basic kitchen appliances, it wasn't ideal, but considering the circumstances, it would do.

Harold's sketchbook and records that he had sent ahead of his trip sat in the corner next to his bag. That was it. Every possession he called his own condensed into the corner of a beige room on the Isle of Galkirk. Harold had never been one for destiny, fate, or believing that life had a set path for everyone, but if he was, he would never have believed that this was what life had in store for him.

He could hear the large group of people outside and remembered that Christian had mentioned that there was some kind of market today. Checking his watch, he could see that it was fast approaching midday, and so he decided he'd best start preparing himself for his new life.

As he left the small shared bathroom at the end of the corridor, a man armed with a toothbrush and wearing only a towel stood towering over him. "I'm sorry. I thought it was empty." The tall man stood slightly hunched over, a large afro sitting on top of his head. The two stood silently for a moment, not knowing what to say. Then, forcing a smile, the tall man spoke again. "I'm Charlie. You're in room 4a, right? I guess we're neighbours." He offered a hand to Harold, careful not to let his towel unravel. "It's Harold, right?"

"Nice to meet you, Charlie. Yeah, I'm in 4a. Sorry if I made a racket last night. I didn't think anyone was awake, so I was just going to sleep downstairs. But then Christian came in and he didn't seem to care for being quiet."

"Ah, don't worry about that. He likes to make a bit of a song and dance whenever we get a new resident. We're used to it by now." Charlie's shoulders dropped, and he seemed more relaxed already. His physique suggested he had once been a very fit man, but time had taken its toll on him. "4a doesn't have a kettle in I don't think. You can borrow mine if you need?"

"That's kind of you, but I think I'm going to head out to the market for a bit. Christian said I should try the chicken rolls or something? I'm hoping they're as good as he says. I'm starving." Charlie seemed to tense up again.

"Oh, yes. The chicken rolls." With that, he darted past Harold into the bathroom and closed the door. Harold wondered if everyone on the island except Christian was that odd. If they were, he wouldn't be making many friends here.

Harold made his way out into the town square and was surprised by how different it looked from last night. Although there was still a thick fog in the air, he could make out at least two dozen market stalls, each one littered with various items and goods. As he took a few steps outside, the smell of cooked meat was even stronger, and soon he could see the stall Christian had talked about. The lady behind the stall, presumably Mrs. Sands, beckoned Harold to come over, with a roll in her hand. Feeling his pockets in the hope of finding his wallet, Mrs. Sands laughed and told him that the chicken rolls were free. Being the first meal Harold had eaten for over twenty-four hours, he was expecting it to taste phenomenal, but to his disappointment, it was bland and tasted like plain chicken.

Looking around the market, Harold made an effort to introduce himself to several of the stall owners. Being a little preoccupied with his new surroundings, he forgot all their names as soon as they'd introduced themselves. All except one.

Manu was an Italian man who wore his hair pulled back into two small buns. He had been selling all manner of smart hats, but none that fit Harold. Harold only remembered Manu's name because the Italian immediately asked if he'd heard of a boy named Trevor, who had seen a UFO in a town Manu lived in for a while. Manu told Harold that it had been national news, and had "put the small town of Haelville, USA on the map!", but Harold hadn't heard of it.

After Harold circled the market for his second look around, he noticed a small stall selling vinyls, and he immediately spotted something that piqued his interest. Kraftwerk's *The Man Machine* and its bright red cover had been a favourite of Harold's before he'd come to Galkirk. It was only small, but he already regretted not bringing it with him.

"I've not seen you here before," said the lady behind the stall with a German accent "are you new?"

"I arrived last night" replied Harold, still looking at the cover. He laid it down and offered a hand to the lady. "I'm Harold."

"Franziska," she replied, shaking his hand "welcome to Galkirk. You're a fan?" She pointed at the record. Her face was thin, with delicate features, and her dark hair reached the small of her back. As she bowed her head to her hands to light a cigarette, Harold noticed that she was missing an ear. "I brought that with me when I came here, I'm sick of it now. Reminds me too much of home," she explained from the side of her mouth.

"That's exactly why I'm interested in it," chuckled Harold.

"You're from Germany?"

"Oh, no. I mean I had it back at home. How much is it?" Franziska took a drag from her cigarette and shrugged.

"Honestly, I didn't even know it was in there. Call it half a token."

"Half a token?" Before Harold could continue, he felt a firm grip on his shoulder. It was Christian. Dressed in the same clothes as last night but looking like he'd slept well, he had a chicken roll in his hand.

"See, as promised," he said with a smile, pointing at the roll. "Half a token, Franzi? That's a steal! Had I known I'd have taken it for my own collection. But, very well, half a token it is. Take mine. And do you still have that one I've been eyeing? The white one with the two fellas on the front?" Franziska pulled out a copy of *Please* and handed it to Christian. "I'll swing by a bit later to pick it up, but I'll pay for now if that's ok. One and a half tokens, right?" Christian handed over a small slip of blue paper, Franziska clipped it twice and handed it back with a wicked smile. Harold could tell there was a past between the two but couldn't tell exactly what. "Always a pleasure, never a chore."

"Tschüss."

Christian picked up the Kraftwerk vinyl, gave it to Harold, and gestured for Harold to follow him. Harold had felt someone looking at him as he was speaking to Franzi and had presumed it was Christian, but he could still feel it. He looked up towards the sea of windows that loomed over him from the buildings surrounding the market. If anybody was watching Harold, he wouldn't easily be able to tell where it was coming from.

As the two strolled around the market, Harold was surprised by just how normal everything was. People were talking, laughing, and interacting with each other. From what he could see, people were happy.

"They say you shouldn't judge a book by its cover, but we all do, even me. So, what's your first impression, Harold? From the little you've seen." It was if Christian could tell exactly what Harold was thinking.

"Well, if I'm honest, it looks... well, normal." Harold looked down at the record he was holding, remembering when Maria had bought it for him.

"You thought an island full of misfits and people that have strayed from God's path wouldn't be?" laughed Christian. "I understand perhaps better than most that having a past doesn't make someone a bad person. I mean, I'm told you met Charlie this morning, did he seem like a bad person to you? Or Franzi?"

"Well, no. But I've only just met them, so that doesn't really give me a good indication as to what they're like as people, does it?"

"Franzi killed a man in self-defence 15 years ago. She came here shortly after, and she's been as good as gold. In the eyes of the law, she's a criminal and nothing more. But here, she gets a fresh start. I did, she did, and now, you do."

"What about Charlie? What did he do?" Christian stopped and turned to face Harold, a hint of frustration in his eyes.

"Listen, the only person who knows what's what around here is me. We accept just about anyone, but you don't discuss your past mistakes. Franzi? She's been vocal in the past and was punished for her mistake. Everyone knows her story, but she's the exception. You don't ask, you don't tell, and you don't share."

Harold looked down to avoid eye contact and remembered how Christian had paid for the record with a blue strip of paper. "Christian, Franzi said this was half a token," he held up the record "what's a token?"

"Tokens are our currency, but they're not physical, they're metaphorical. You see, when you work a full day, you get 6 tokens. If you don't work, you don't get any tokens. I'd have thought someone with your qualifications could have worked that out?" laughed Christian.

"I presumed that. What I meant was how do I get tokens? I don't have a job?"

"You'll want to speak to The Hermit about that, down that way." He pointed to a path that spiraled away from the town square. "Little brown house on the left, you can't miss it. The fella keeps to himself, so we don't see too much of him. I'd recommend treating him like an animal in a cage. Look at him from a distance, but don't stick your head in. He might bite off your nose!" Harold tried his best to keep the conversation serious.

"What about my rent, how many tokens is that?"

"Don't you worry about that, Harry. I've got you all covered in that department."

"But why?" questioned Harold "Surely there's something I can do?"

"There will be. But for now, don't worry about it." Christian began to walk back towards the building where Harold was staying. Looking back over his shoulder, he shouted: "But those chicken rolls, huh? Fantastic!"

The fog made it hard to see far along the path that Christian had pointed out, but Harold was curious. As he made his way along the path, the sounds from the market began to fade, and before long it was eerily quiet. As he passed some small houses, he noticed various pieces of fishing equipment attached to the outside walls. Mainly nets, with a few buoys and rods. Every house seemed to have them, and Harold wondered if fishing was still a big part of the island. Considering chicken wasn't exactly commonly found at sea, he wondered how the island managed to get their supply. He began to wonder how they got most of their supplies: the hats Manu sold, the records from Franziska, everything.

Before he could think too much about it, he'd arrived at the brown house. It looked significantly older than the others from the outside but had no fishing decorations. Harold knocked twice on the door but decided to let himself in when he heard no response. The feeling of someone watching him had gone, but Harold kept his guard up.

Inside the house, the decoration certainly made up for the lack of exterior design. Hunching over to avoid the lobster cages hanging from the low ceiling, Harold could see all manner of items. From dockers hooks and empty barrels to aprons and kitchenware, there was a little bit of everything. Ahead of him was a small wooden desk, and a sign reading 'everything for sale'. Harold called out and knocked on the desk but heard no response. Next to the desk was an old record player paced on top of a pile of books. It looked worse for wear, but in good enough condition to play his new record. As he crouched down for a closer look, he heard rustling from the room behind the desk. He reached up and placed the record onto the desk to inspect the record player.

"Kraftwerk? I don't sell that rubbish here! Where did you find this? Bet is was that German girl on the market. Filipa or Francisco or something." The husky voice came from behind the desk. As Harold stood up with the record player in hand, his eyes were fixed firmly on the machine.

"Hey, I don't have any tokens yet, but how much is this?" Harold looked at the man behind the desk, dropping the record player onto the desk without even noticing.

"Harold? Harold Kobbs, is that really you?"

Chapter 3:
Franziska.

"Manu, I don't mean to be rude, but this is all a load of shit."

"Well, you'd know about wearing shit, wouldn't you Yvette?"

"Try it, pasta boy."

Yvette and Manu had always had a strange relationship. They had the kind of connection that meant they could rip into each other and know they meant nothing by it. To the others around them though, it seemed as if the pair could bust out into a brawl at any moment. "Enough chit chat, where's my order?"

"You know it's not here yet, you weird girl, so stop busting my balls and ask the captain where it is. Or will you finally admit you're just asking so you can talk to me?" Yvette cracked a smile.

"Come off it, Manu. Everybody knows you're sweet on Franzi." With that, Manu made sure his hair was presentable and started looking around frantically.

"Is she looking? Is she looking this way?" Manu looked over to Franzi. She noticed the Italian looking at her and pretended to turn the other way. Then, with a jolt, she turned back to face him, pulling the ugliest face she could. Her hair was tucked behind her ears, and her eyes were crossed.

Yvette winked at the Italian before continuing to browse the market. Rain was in the air, but most of the residents had become used to the weather by now, and didn't let it ruin their weekly market. However, it was late in the day, and as the rain picked up, Yvette decided her day at the market was done. She headed into the red brick building, expecting the last few stall owners to follow behind her soon.

Closing the heavy wooden door behind her, she felt the heat of the room hit her smack in the face. At least half of the residents were already in their seats, and as Yvette ordered herself a drink, Christian climbed onto a chair to address everybody in the room.

"Thank you for coming, everybody. We're just waiting for the last few residents to close the market and make their way inside. Michael, if you could give those outside a shout, we'll get started." Yvette grabbed her drink and took her seat next to Charlie.

"Find anything good today?" asked Charlie, his large hands laid face-down on the table.

"Not today. Manu still doesn't have the hat I've ordered, but I was expecting that."

"Has he spoken to Franzi yet? He realises this is a small place, right? Word travels fast." Christian was still stood on the chair, his skinny frame somehow managing to captivate the residents without him saying a word.

Franzi, Manu, and the rest of the market soon made their way into the room. With only a few spare seats remaining, Manu elected to give up his usual space for Franzi with Charlie and Yvette nudging each other as he did so.

"Thank you, everybody. Just a few quick words, then we can call it an evening." By now, Christian had made his way from his chair over to the bar. With all eyes on him, he began to address the crowd in his usual, charismatic way. "As you know, we've got a new resident arriving in a couple of weeks. His name is Harold, and he'll be taking Mr. Sands' old room. 4a, is it?" He looked towards Charlie who nodded in reply. "Yes, 4a. Which reminds me, we'll be having a memorial service for Mr. Sands tomorrow at 3 on the dock. He will be missed and remembered fondly by us all, but let his passing remind you all of the dangers of straying past Doctor Halter's house. I've told you all before that this area has not been cleared by us, and therefore should not be entered by anyone. We were lucky to recover his body and bury him at sea before Mrs. Sands could see the state it was in." The room fell eerily silent, with everybody hanging on Christian's every word.

"Anyway, back to our new resident. You all remember the rules, so please stick to them for when he arrives. We all know what it's like when you arrive here at Galkirk, so let's try and make him as comfortable as possible. With regards to the rules, Franzi, would you come up here please?" Franzi looked reluctant to do so but Christian beckoned her with an open hand, so she rose out of her chair and made her way to the bar. "Franzi, when you came here, we took you under our wing, we made you part of our family, and you were aware of the rules. Now, it has come to my attention that you've been talking about your past. I respect that you're embracing this, and you don't wish for it to consume you. However, you know the rules, and have agreed to accept the consequences of your actions, correct?" Franzi nodded, with a hint of fear in her eyes. "Good. And you trust me?" She nodded again. "Good, then please, put this over your eyes, and lay flat on the bar."

Christian presented a blindfold to Franzi. She tied it around her head, and felt her way up onto the bar, laying down flat with her head to the side, facing the back. Christian turned her head so that she was facing the residents of the island, before tying her hands behind her back and her feet together. Christian turned to face the audience and pulled out a pocketknife. He showed it to the residents as if he were a stage magician and climbed onto the bar to straddle Franzi. Pulling a cloth out of the other pocket, he stuffed it into Franzi's mouth and flicked open the pocketknife. Charlie raised his large hands to his eyes to shield them from seeing what Christian was about to do, but as Christian approached the side of Franzi's head, he took one last look at the audience. "Ladies and gentlemen, this is a punishment not only for our resident German here but for you as well for not reiterating the rules to her. So, please, refrain from covering your eyes, or else I'll have to do the other side, too." As Charlie dropped his hands, tears were starting to form. "Thank you," grinned Christian.

Turning back to Franzi, he placed the knife behind her ear. As he began to slice, Franzi's scream was muffled by the cloth in her mouth, which made it all the more harrowing. As the residents covered their mouths and watched through tear-filled eyes, Christian began to pinch the ear upwards to get a cleaner cut. As blood began to pour down the side of Franzi's face, Christian continued to cut. After a few smooth slices, he aggressively jabbed the knife up and down, causing blood to spurt over himself and the bar. After a few more downwards motions, the ear had come off. "Doctor Halter, if you please," said Christian, looking at the severed ear. As the doctor hastily left his seat to attend to Franzi, Christian climbed off the bar and made his way over to the seat he'd stood on moments ago. As Christian strolled through the residents, he stuffed the ear into his pocket along with the pocketknife, with Franzi still screaming whilst the doctor attended to her.

"It doesn't get any easier, does it?" Yvette whispered to Charlie, but as she looked over to the mountain of a man beside her, she saw he was still in shock. He sat with his hands over his mouth, staring desperately at Franzi. Yvette looked behind her to find Manu but was surprised to see he was just leaning casually against the wall, looking down at his feet. As Christian climbed back onto the chair, all eyes turned to him again.

"So, as I said, his name is Harold, and he will be here soon. Thank you for your time."

Chapter 4:
Threads.

With a scarred chin and a nose that bent slightly to the left, there was no mistaking him. It might have been several years since he saw him last, but stood in front of Harold now with his small stature and bushy eyebrows was Jerry Jones, the man that had inspired Harold to become a teacher.

"Harold Kobbs, that can't really be you, can it? What are you doing here?"

"Mr. Jones, you look- well, you look-"

"Broken? Ill? Like I've lost the will to live?" Jerry had always looked a bit worse for wear, due to the amateur boxing tournaments he participated in as a young man. Although it had been at least 15 years since Harold last saw him, he didn't expect him to look quite this bad. His eyes were gaunt with large bags underneath, and where there was once a stocky frame was now a skinny, wiry man with clothes that hung off him like a child in its parent's clothing. His large hands with sausage-like fingers were now thin and bony, and if it hadn't been for the chin and nose, Harold would have questioned if this could really be the same man that had inspired him all those years ago.

"You look different," Harold said. The two stood looking at each other for a moment, soaking in the silence. Harold tried desperately to think of something to say, and managed to muster

"Christian said to come here to look for work?" Jerry's expression soon changed from shock to a deep sense of concern.

"What do you mean?" The old man's eyes started darting up and down, assessing Harold. "Wait, you're not the new resident, are you?"

"Yes, I arrived yesterday." Jerry placed his hands together and raised them to his face. He began to frown as he shook his head, making sure to cover his eyes.

"Harold, no. What happened? What did you do?" Jerry said through his hands, his voice trembling with every word.

"Jerry, Christian said not to talk about that stuff. But it's really good to see you. Maybe we can catch up soon an-"

"No, silly bollocks! What did you do?" Jerry slammed his hands onto the desk, his eyes now struggling to hold back the tears. "You arrived yesterday! You need to tell me right now what you did!"

"Jerry, I don't understand."

Before he could reply, Jerry was startled by a crashing sound from the room behind him.

"Don't move," he told Harold with an outstretched finger "not a muscle! There are things you need to know before you get too settled here". He crept into the back room, pulling the door to behind him.

Harold had always been bad at containing his curiosity, and it often overshadowed both his sense and his reason. So, it was no surprise that almost immediately, he ignored his old friend's command and began to look around the shop. Ducking under hanging objects and squeezing through tight gaps proved fruitless, as he found nothing of interest. He was still interested in the record player and hoped his friend would allow him to take it with him on the promise of tokens to come. Harold eventually made his way back to the desk, hoping to see or hear some sign of his friend's return, but there was nothing.

Moseying behind the desk, curiosity once again got the better of Harold, and he began to rummage through the drawers of the desk. It wasn't in Harold's nature to look through other people's private possessions, but he had grown impatient in his friend's absence.

Just when he thought he was going to have no luck in finding something interesting, the back of Harold's hand brushed against what felt like the leather cover of a book. It felt as if it was stuck to the roof of the drawer, hidden away from anyone nosey enough to search it. Harold peeled it away and stood looking at it for a moment before noticing the discolouration of his knuckle on his right thumb. He had never been the type to engage in physical violence, and it showed. Since he'd had to pop the bone back into its socket a few days ago, the colour had turned to a nasty, dark purple. Harold made a mental note to never attempt fight moves he'd seen in movies again - especially if they involved your adversary's eyes.

Harold opened the leather-bound book he held in his hands, and it fell to a page with a Polaroid picture stuck to it. There were two people in the photograph; Jerry and a young blonde woman, caught mid-laughter in what looked like the square on a market day. On the white section below the photograph, someone had written "Yvette and me, 1982". Flicking through the pages, there were no other photographs, just scribblings, and drawings. Harold turned back to the photograph for a closer look. He hadn't seen the woman at the market earlier that day and wondered how many of the other residents he hadn't met yet.

Realising it had been some time since he'd seen Jerry, Harold closed the book and placed it on top of the record player on the desk.

"Jerry?" called Harold, but there was no response. Harold realised he hadn't heard any sound since his friend had disappeared into the back room and decided to investigate it for himself. To his surprise, there was nobody there, it was just a storeroom. There was a small window, perhaps big enough for his friend to fit through, but no doors other than the one Harold was stood in. His friend had vanished.

Looking around for some indication as to where Jerry had gone, Harold noticed a small, folded piece of paper on the floor. Scribbled inside was the message 'take the record player, my treat – Jerry'. It didn't resemble the neat handwriting from inside the leather book, instead it looked sloppy and rushed.

Harold didn't sleep at all that night. Thoughts of his old friend and what had happened kept running through in his head. What had Jerry been so worried about? Where had he gone in such a rush? Harold wondered if coming to the island had been a mistake – a mistake he couldn't rectify now even if he'd tried. There was no going back.

It was the early hours, too early to play his new record. As Harold laid on his bed, he wondered why Jerry had even been on the island. He knew he wasn't supposed to be concerned with people's past here, but Jerry had always seemed like a good person. If he'd done something bad to end up on the island, it must have been extremely out of character.

Harold then began to wonder if people back home had realised he'd gone. It had all happened so fast; before he knew it, he'd kissed Maria goodbye in her sleep, taken his bags, and left. As far as they knew, he'd disappeared without a trace after the incident, but in reality, he was on a rainy, foggy island not that far from home in the hopes of escaping his past.

Harold thought about drawing to distract himself, but as he sat up in his bed, he heard someone talking to themselves in the town square outside. He peered out of the small window in his room to see that Manu was sat on the fountain in the middle of the square trying, and failing, to light a cigarette. Seeing an opportunity to get some answers, Harold put on his shoes and pulled a t-shirt over his head, careful to avoid his eye in the process. He made his way out of his room, down the stairs, and into the square.

Noticing how fast Harold was moving, Manu raised an eyebrow in Harold's direction.

"Someone is desperate for a smoke, eh? You quit recently or something?"

"Manu," Harold panted "we need to talk. Where can we go that's private?" Manu finally managed to light his cigarette. He took a large drag on it and exhaled through his nose, almost as if he wasn't phased by the encounter.

"A secret island's not private enough for you?" Manu wasn't the kind of person Harold had expected to find on the island. He seemed like he hadn't a care in the world, and apart from their first encounter with talk of UFOs, he seemed very down to earth. The Italian gestured with his head towards the building opposite where Harold was staying, and soon they were inside.

The interior of the building was extremely dull. The wallpaper was plain non-invasive, and all the furniture was a bland beige colour, making it look a little like a retirement home. Harold followed Manu up to the third floor and into the his room. Apart from the double bed and a few pictures on the wall, it looked much the same as Harold's. A guitar sat in the corner, covered in dust, and hairbands littered the small table set up in the corner. Manu cracked the window open and pulled a chair over to it, continuing to smoke the cigarette he'd lit outside. "Go ahead, little man," said Manu, looking at Harold. Harold assumed this was how Manu spoke to people he didn't know too well, considering Harold was anything but short

"Manu, do you know Jerry? In the little brown house away from the market?" Manu looked at Harold with an air of confusion. "Christian called him The Hermit?"

"Oh, The Hermit! Yes, I know him. Why?"

"I was speaking to him yesterday. One minute he was there, and the next he was gone," said Harold as fast as he could.

"He disappeared in front of your eyes?"

"Well, no. I was talking to him, then he went into the storeroom and then he was gone."

"How odd." Manu didn't seem too phased by what Harold had told him.

"Look, if you're not interested in helping me, that's fine. All I need is for you to tell me how I can find someone called Yvette." With that, Manu's eyes snapped to meet Harold's.

"Yvette? Why?"

"There's a picture of her with Jerry in a book I found in the store. Jerry is an old friend from years ago, but we lost contact." Manu laughed before tapping his cigarette out of the window.

"Good luck finding Yvette."

"Why?"

"She's, how do you say, 'M.I.A.' too. I last saw her about a week ago, which, on an island as small as this is a long time my friend."

"You act as if people going missing is a part of everyday life."

Manu flicked his cigarette out of the window and stood to face Harold.

"My friend, people come to Galkirk to leave the past behind, but there are some demons you cannot outrun, no matter how hard you try. And demons make people do crazy things, like running away to an island for misfits. But in the end, you either come to terms with your demons, or they get the better of you."

Manu began to re-tie his hair into the small buns Harold had seen him with yesterday. "When people disappear from Galkirk, well," he shrugged "you know." Harold slumped onto Manu's bed, trying to comprehend what he'd heard. Now more than ever he was doubting his decision to leave everything behind, wondering if he'd have been better off facing the consequences of his actions.

Noticing his defeated look, Manu took a seat next to him. Lighting up another cigarette, he offered one to Harold, who quickly declined. The Italian placed a hand on Harold's shoulder and began to look at the pictures on his wall. "It's not easy, leaving it all behind. But listen, you find one or two people here you can trust, and that you like, and it'll soon become home. After all, you don't get this size of room in a prison block!" he joked.

"Is it worth it though?" questioned Harold. Manu shrugged again, still looking at the various Polaroids and pictures.

"Well, my country doesn't exactly look fondly upon those that have committed crimes against children, but what can I say? If you try to break into my house, I will shoot."

"Jesus. Were they trying to steal from you?"

"Mmm no, I think they were looking for their ball in my yard or something."

Before Harold could respond, there were three light taps at the door, almost as if whoever was responsible feared to wake Manu. As the Italian opened the door Harold could see it was Franziska, the woman from the vinyl stall. The two spoke so quietly that Harold couldn't make out what they were saying, but before long Manu had held the door open for Franziska, and the three of them were all cramped inside of Manu's room.

"Harold," Franziska said tentatively "how are you?"

"He's a bit shaken," said Manu before Harold had a chance to reply, "he's friends with The Hermit, but he's gone missing."

"Oh wow, he made friends quickly. He's been here, what, two days? And already making friends. That's got to be a record."

"Am I going completely fucking insane?" shouted Harold, likely waking the neighbours in the process.

"Jesus. Calm down, little man."

"No, I will not fucking calm down, *little man*," Harold said patronisingly. "Two people have disappeared recently and you two act so fucking nonchalantly about it! Why is this not a big deal to you two?" Harold was now stood upright, his arms outstretched as if he were addressing an audience.

"Two people?" Franziska turned to Manu, "What did you tell him?"

"I told him about Yvette, why?"

"Right," interrupted Harold, "you two sit down and tell me everything you know about these missing people. I'm not leaving here until you tell me everything. Who's disappeared, when they disappeared, and anything else you know about them." Harold leaned his back against the door in an effort to block the exit, but Franziska and Manu couldn't care less. They casually sat on the bed and told him everything they knew.

The stories of all the missing residents filled Harold's head with questions, so much so that he slumped to the floor with his back still against the door. When Manu had finished speaking, silence filled the room, the eeriness of which lead the Italian to start biting his nails. Franziska quickly slapped his hand from his mouth, telling him it was a bad habit.

"What about Christian? What do you know about him?" questioned Harold.

"No," snapped Franziska, making her way towards the open window, "no more, we shouldn't be talking about this stuff."

"Why not? People are going missing an-"

"This is why!" Franziska pulled her hair behind her head, revealing a scarred and stitched stub of an ear. It looked like whatever had happened to Franziska's ear had happened recently. Harold assumed that, because of the stitching, it had also been tended to professionally. "This is what happens to people who talk about their past."

"What do you mean?"

"Christian," said Manu in a low voice.

"Christian did that? Why?"

"He told you not to ask questions about the past, right? This is what he does when you do," Franziska managed, holding back the tears. Seeing her distress, Manu made his way to Franziska and embraced her. Seeing the agony he'd caused, Harold apologised, raising his hand to his mouth as he did.

"This is why we don't ask questions, my friend. We've come here to start fresh, not cause more trouble." Manu looked at Harold with sad eyes. Despite only meeting him yesterday, this was a side of Manu that Harold hadn't expected to see. The once confident, care-free man now looked scared.

"Living in fear is no life at all," said Harold confidently. "I'm sorry that this has happened to you, Franziska, but I can't just let this go. Jerry is my friend, and he might be in trouble."

"I understand," said the Italian, lighting a cigarette for both Franziska and himself, "But I need you to know that we won't be a part of it." Harold nodded in agreement.

"There's just one more thing I need from you. Which room was Yvette's?"

"Downstairs, room 11," managed Franziska from one side of her mouth, the cigarette hanging out of the other. Harold placed a hand on the doorknob, ready to leave. Before he could twist it open though, Manu had placed something in Harold's other hand: an envelope addressed to Manu, with some small object inside.

"This might help you," he said whilst Harold looked over his shoulder at the couple, "but please, you can't tell anyone about Franzi and me. It's for the best." Franziska looked at Harold, her eyes asking the same.

"Thank you," said Harold, closing the door behind him.

Harold made his way downstairs to find room 11. He passed only one person on his way; a woman with an afro not too dissimilar to Charlie's, who didn't so much as look at Harold. After a few minutes of searching, Harold found it. He tried the doorknob, but the door was locked shut. Feeling the envelope between his finger and thumb, Harold could tell there was a key inside, along with a letter. He tried the key in the lock of room 11, and sure it enough, it opened. Closing the door carefully behind him, he hesitated before locking it from the inside.

The room looked much the same as Harold's and Manu's, leading Harold to believe that every room on the island looked the same. He began to wonder who had built it all and where they were now but decided not to dwell on it. The only difference between this room and the one's Harold had seen before was the untidiness. Pictures and scraps of paper littered every surface, seemingly with no order. T-shirts and bras were sprawled out on the floor, and the whole room looked as if it had been ransacked. Trying his best not to step on anything but the floor, Harold tiptoed around the mess, hoping to find something of use. After a while of attempting to preserve the chaos, he gave up and began to trample over the clothes. Harold's curious nature got the better of him once more, and soon he found himself rummaging through Yvette's drawers and desk. Much like the room itself, the drawers were a mess, filled with a haphazard mixture of clothing, books, and other random objects. Harold remembered how he had found the book in Jerry's desk and tried the roofs of the drawers. To his surprise, he found another leather-bound book. This one was a dark red, with just a few of the pages written in. A similar picture of Yvette and Jerry, which appeared to have been taken the same day as the one in Jerry's book, had been stuck onto the inside cover. Harold wondered what kind of relationship the two had had, and if it had been the reason the two were now missing.

Flicking through the opening pages, Harold saw nothing of interest. It looked as though it had been an ordinary diary, with times, dates, and short descriptions of what Yvette had been doing. As Harold got to the last entry in the book, just a few pages in, he saw that it was dated only ten days before Harold had arrived. The short description underneath read: *"Found a weird, old building away from the square. Looked like an old factory building or something. Spoke to Jerry about it, but he told me it was nothing. Will take a look tonight."* Harold closed the book, and took one last look around the room, but found nothing of interest.

He closed the door behind him and locked it after ensuring that the chaos inside the room was somewhat similar to how he'd left it. He'd made up his mind; he'd have to investigate the building that Yvette had found, but he'd have to do it when nobody was about. Aware that he'd have to put some time between Jerry's disappearance and finding the building to avoid any unnecessary attention, he decided he'd go the following night. Until then he'd have to blend in and act normal, but before anything else, he'd go to the privacy of his room and read what was in Yvette's letter to Manu.

Chapter 5:
Curiosity.

Yvette pulled up her jeans and zipped up the fly. As she looked over her shoulder at Charlie, she noticed he was still in a deep sleep, which usually happened after a night together. Pulling the diary from the first drawer on the left, she pencilled in a quick entry reading only: *January 4th, 1984 - It still surprises me how small a big man can be.* She slid the diary into the back pocket of her jeans, stuffed the key to her room in a plain envelope, and left it on the table, careful not to wake the giant lying fast asleep in her bed.

Making her way to the town square, Yvette passed a few of her neighbours in the thin corridor of her building. Max, Taylor, and Josiah all said their usual greetings as they passed, but Yvette was surprised that Felix didn't flash his usual morning smile. He seemed preoccupied, barely noticing that they'd passed. Yvette hoped he was fine, and wanted to ask, but knew that with Felix, it was best not to.

As Yvette stepped into the open square, the chill of the fresh morning air engulfed her entire body, sending shivers down her spine and causing little goosebumps to appear on her arms. With the sky a gloomy grey colour and a thin layer of fog hanging in the air, it was about as nice as it could be at that time of year. Taking a glance at her watch, she saw that she was earlier than usual, so she decided to take it slow, observing the old buildings and few people around her. As she took a seat on the edge of the stone fountain in the middle of the square, she realised that although she had been on the island for nearly two years now, she always found something new when she looked hard enough.

As she approached Jerry's shop, she knocked twice, and within a few moments Jerry opened the door, his arms outstretched to meet her.

"Good morning, Yvette!" he said joyfully, "You're early today, huh? Couldn't sleep?"

"Quite the opposite," she replied as she stepped through the doorway, "I had an early night." Jerry looked her, knowing the answer before he'd even asked.

"Charlie?"

"Charlie."

"He's a good guy, Yvette. I don't like that whole arrangement between you two. You know he'll get too attached." Yvette ignored him and made her way to the small kitchen area at the back of the shop. Making herself a coffee to warm up, she offered one to Jerry, which he gladly accepted.

The two went about their usual business for the day, taking stock and filling in order requests for the captain, with a sprinkling of customers throughout. By closing time, Jerry was holding his lower back, complaining that he'd never felt that way when he was teaching before he moved to the island. Yvette joked that it was because he was old, and the two shared a laugh. They were always laughing and joking around each other. Unexpectedly, Yvette had taken to Jerry in a way the other residents hadn't, and she saw him much like the father she'd always wanted. Someone she could go to for advice when she needed it, and someone to share their concern when she did something foolish.

"What are you up to tonight?" asked Jerry, "Anything fun?"

"I'm thinking of going for a walk up that way," she said as she pointed away from the town square, "I've not ventured very far that way. I thought I'd give it a go." Jerry tilted his head to the side, as he often did when he didn't agree with something.

"I know that if I tell you not to, you'll do it anyway. But please, don't go too far. You know Christian doesn't allow residents to venture too far outside of the town."

"I'll be fine," she said, placing her hands on his shoulders, "You know what I'm like."

"That's exactly why I'm worried," he replied.

Yvette said her goodbyes to Jerry and hugged him once more, before setting off on the path away from the town.

As she found herself surrounded by small houses she hadn't seen before, she reached to the back pocket of her jeans but was confused as to why she couldn't find her diary. As she searched the cobbled path around her for the book, she noticed a pair of smart shoes attached to skinny legs behind her. It was Christian.

"Good evening, Yvette. Out for a stroll?" His hands were behind his back, and he was dressed in a pink button-down shirt, with dark blue suit trousers. Yvette had always wondered what Christian's job had been before he'd come to the island, as he was always dressed like a banker or businessman. He was clean-shaven, and had a face for it, with cheekbones and a jawline to die for.

"Christian, how are you?" Ignoring the question, Christian cracked a smile.

"I'm just letting everyone know that there's a bit of a delay with our new resident. The captain wrote to me to let me know that he's having trouble getting hold of this 'Harold' fella."

"Oh, that's a shame," said Yvette, "I hope he's OK."

"Likewise, but it's out of our hands. It's like wandering into the unknown. There are things you can't control, no matter how hard you try. You can't be prepared for everything." Yvette wondered if Christian knew about her plan to explore parts of the island, or if it had been a coincidence.

"Yes," Yvette said hesitantly, "well, I best be going." Before she could turn her back on Christian, he revealed her diary from behind his back. He held it out in front of him with a mischievous look upon his face, looking like a child holding back a secret.

"I found this on the fountain this morning. You should be more careful." As Yvette reached for the diary, he pulled her hand towards him and held her close, her ear close to his mouth. "People act strangely when somebody finds out their secrets," he whispered menacingly, "you never quite know how they'll react." He reached around Yvette and slid the diary into her back pocket, before stepping away and walking back towards the square. Yvette thought for sure that he'd read her diary and was frustrated with herself for being so foolish. She made a mental note to adopt Jerry's way of hiding books, by sticking them to the roof of a drawer, and continued on her way towards the unknown.

By now it was getting dark, and she hadn't come across any houses or small buildings for some time. The cobblestone path had ended, and she found herself stood on wet grassland, with what seemed like a dirt path leading into a woodland area. It didn't look dense or hard to walk through, but the lack of light and the mud underfoot would complicate things. Looking up, she could see a powerline leading into and possibly past the woodland area. This was the reason she'd come looking. She'd noticed it a few days ago, but the people she'd asked - mainly Jerry and Charlie - had no knowledge of what could need power out this far. There was a chance it was something as simple as a generator, or even nothing at all, but Yvette couldn't contain her curiosity and began to make her way into the woods.

As she pushed back low-hanging branches and stepped over fallen logs, she was reminded of her childhood. As a little girl, she used to go exploring with the neighbour's son, who was of a similar age. He was a scout at the time, and he'd always be giving Yvette tips on how to survive in the wilderness that she'd likely never use. He'd taught her to always look for bent branches and broken sticks underfoot, as that meant you were on the right path, and so she did.

The sounds of seagulls squawking and twigs snapping beneath her feet gave way to distant rumblings, the likes of which she hadn't heard since before she moved to the island. Step by step, the low rumbling became a much louder, industrial noise, almost like the sound of heavy machinery. as Light was breaking through the trees towards Yvette, coming from the same direction as the ominous sound. As she approached the light, she could see an opening ahead, free of trees and woodland.

Taking cover behind the trunk of a large tree, Yvette peered into the clearing. In its centre, surrounded by the woodland on every side, was a single factory building, which looked to be in full operation. The cold, grey metal and brick structure stood around three storeys tall, with a jagged and corrugated roof. A bright yellow light pierced through the few windows of the building and darted out into the surrounding woodland. At one end Yvette could see a handful of people in long blue aprons stood around a doorway, chatting to each other. Yvette didn't recognise any of them, but the distance between them and her made it difficult. After a few minutes of studying the building, Yvette spotted two more figures in the same blue aprons dragging a large sack towards the group. Whatever was inside looked heavy and took both men dragging it together to move it at a comfortable pace. The two new arrivals stopped briefly to speak to the group outside the doorway before two others helped carry the sack into the building. Yvette tried to scribble an entry in her diary but realised that she hadn't brought a pen or pencil with her, and even if she had, the light wasn't bright enough to write clearly. She studied the group a while longer until they made their way inside the building, where the machinery fired up once again. Waiting for something else to happen, Yvette stayed firmly behind the tree trunk, but there was no movement. She wondered if there was another entrance around the other side of the building, but she couldn't risk checking it now, as it was getting too dark. She decided to come back a little earlier the following day so she could use the natural light to study the building further. She tucked the diary back into her pocket, and carefully made her way back to the town.

Yvette awoke the next morning to the sound of rain crashing against her window. She had become used to the rain since moving to the island, but it was exceptionally heavy today. She could barely see the square's fountain of the square outside her window, which was perfect for continuing her snoop around the factory from the night before. She wrote a quick entry into her diary, describing the previous night's events, and stuck it to the roof of her drawer. She'd showered the night before so that she could get a quicker start today, and she'd barely got her jeans on before making her towards the door.

As she was about to leave, she paused. Something came over her. She wasn't sure what it was, but she couldn't leave just yet. Pushing the mess of clothes and paper off her desk onto the floor, she took a seat and began to write. By the time she'd finished, she realised the letter wasn't addressed to anyone but was written as if it was. Who could she write to? Who did she trust enough to give the letter to? She thought about addressing it to Jerry, but she decided that'd be too obvious. She settled on addressing the letter 'To Manu', and ran it upstairs, sliding it under Manu's door before heading out.

It wasn't until she'd run all the way to Jerry's that she realised she hadn't brought a coat with her, and by the time she began pounding on Jerry's door, she was soaked through.

"Yvette?" said Jerry as he opened the door. "Jesus, what's wrong with you, girl? You look like a drowned rat! Get yourself inside, you'll catch a damn cold like that."

"No time," managed Yvette as she caught her breath, "I need to borrow a coat. I've found something in the woods, I'm going to check it out!"

"Found something? Like what?" Jerry reached for an old coat of his and handed it to Yvette, wondering what good it'd do her now.

"A building, like a factory! I'll let you know all about it tonight. Cover for me today, please? Tell them I'm ill or something."

"Fine, but you owe me. And please be safe, Yvette. I mean it." Yvette offered Jerry a quick hug, which he politely declined. She threw the coat on and started down the road to the woods. As she made her way along the same path as the night before, Yvette shielded her eyes from the rain. The trees weren't offering much shelter, and soon Yvette began to slip in the mud beneath her feet.

Before long, she found herself at the same clearing as before, and in front of her stood the same menacing block of metal and stone, but this time there was no sign of life inside. The sound of the rain hitting the trees around her made it hard to hear much else, but there was definitely no sound coming from inside the building. Making her way towards where she'd seen the group of people last night, Yvette could see that they'd taken the large sack through a large double-door entrance, which was now padlocked shut. She tried her luck in opening it by hand but was met by the expected result of the door remaining shut. The rain wasn't letting up, and Yvette knew she'd either have to get herself inside or give up on her investigation. Deep down, she knew which one it'd be before she'd even finished thinking the question.

Looking around, she noticed that the windows of the building seemed to be of an old style, where they're held on a single hinge in the middle of the glass and opened by pushing them from the bottom. They were up a little higher than she could reach though, so she'd need some kind of elevation. Luckily, she found a fallen branch on the edges of the woodland area surrounding the factory, which she wedged between the ground and the factory wall. Yvette was worried that the ground would be too muddy, but as she gingerly made her way up the wedged branch, she managed to dig her nails under the window, and, to her surprise, it opened outward. The gap was small, but enough for her to climb inside. Not thinking about what she would be met with when she did, she pulled herself up and through the window, falling onto a hard metal surface on the other side. Despite the pain from the fall, she couldn't have been happier with herself. She'd made it inside the mystery building.

Pulling up her jeans and taking off Jerry's coat, she looked at her surroundings, confused as to why everything was so clean. Just a few hours ago, several people had been working inside, with the machinery sounding as though it was on. However, looking at it now, it was spotlessly clean, as if it'd just been built. There was no sign of it having *ever* been used, let alone less than 24 hours ago.

Inside the factory were several pieces of equipment that Yvette didn't recognise, but they all looked heavy and dangerous. She looked around to find any sign of life, or of the machinery having been used, but found nothing. If the equipment had been operated the night before, it had been scrubbed and cleaned to near-perfect condition afterward. Even the small drain system running beneath her feet was spotless as if it'd never been used.

Before she could take a closer look, she was startled by the sound of the padlocked double doors bursting open. It was Standing there was Christian, dressed as smart as ever, with a small group of people behind him.

"It's funny, isn't it? You set up a slaughterhouse near a farm, and the lambs don't bat an eyelid. Yet you put one far away from a town, and one little townsfolk happens to end up finding it."

"Christian, I'm sorry. I was just curious, and it's not exactly-"

"No," interrupted Christian, his hand raised as if to tell her to stop talking, "I'm the sorry one. I wish it could have been one of the residents I didn't like. I have to say, I know you have your arrangements with Charlie, but I've always liked you. I was even going to try and set you up with this new guy, Harold. You know, mix things up a bit." Christian took off his suit jacket and rolled up his sleeves. "But oh well, I guess I'll have to find someone else for him." Yvette started to step backwards slowly, as Christian made his way towards one of the cabinets on the wall. He unlocked it, pulled out a cleaver, and started towards Yvette, his eyes fixated onto hers.

"Christian, what are you doing?"

"What we do to lambs that stray too far from the herd."

Not wanting to lose sight of him, Yvette continued to move backwards, but after just a few steps, she realised Christian had backed her into a corner, and there was nothing within arm's reach that could help her.

"Christian, stop it, you're scaring me."

"Good," he replied coldly, his eyes fixed on her like a predator stalking its prey. He raised the cleaver high into the air, and as Yvette raised her hands to meet it in the hope of protecting herself, he struck a heavy blow downwards, cutting straight through her fingers and into her head. Yvette's body dropped to the floor; the cleaver still deeply embedded into her skull. As her body lay twitching and convulsing, Christian placed his shoe on her face and withdrew the cleaver from her skull like Excalibur from the stone, then swung his arm downwards once again, the blood spurting onto Christian's face and shirt.

"For fuck's sake! I knew I should have worn an old shirt." He turned to face the group of people that had gathered behind him. "Get to work," said Christian, as he dropped the clever beside the no longer twitching body of Yvette, "and make it quick, I want to continue with my painting today."

Chapter 6:
Bonds.

Harold was stuck in two minds as to whether he should read the letter now, or wait until the next day just before he'd set off to find the building Yvette mentioned in her diary. Catching a glimpse of himself in the mirror of his room, he could see that his beard had started to grow back. His beard had always grown through quickly, and with all of the events since his arrival to the island, he had forgotten to shave. His eye was still dark around the edge but now hurt less than when he'd arrived. Looking down at his hands, he noticed the discolouration of his knuckle was now at its worst – purple, with small areas of yellow piercing through. So much had changed in a short period of time. Just six months ago, Harold had been a happy man with a simple life, a steady job, and Maria. Now, he had almost nothing.

A sharp knock came from Harold's door, startling him and causing him to tuck the letter under his bedsheets before answering. To Harold's surprise, the boat captain stood at his door. With his greying beard all but hiding his mouth, it was his large eyes that showed Harold that the captain seemed happy to see him.

"Mr. Kobbs, good to see you! How are you settling in?"

"Fine," replied Harold tentatively, "how are you?"

"I'm good, I'm good. Just stopping off for a bit to drop off some supplies. I thought I'd come and see how Galkirk's newest resident is getting on." The captain took it upon himself to take a seat at

Harold's desk, producing a small flask from his coat pocket and taking a swig.

"Is there something I can help you with?" asked Harold. It wasn't until now that he'd realised everybody called this man the captain. Not once had he heard anyone give him a proper name.

"I'm actually here to ask you the same thing," came the reply from behind the greying beard, "anything you want?"

"What do you mean?"

"From home," said the captain, cheerily, "any foods or treats or anything you're missing?" Harold thought for a moment, but nothing sprung to mind. He asked the captain if it was allowed, as he was under the impression that the residents were to have no contact with the outside world. The captain replied with a shrug as if he wasn't bothered. At that, Harold had an idea.

"What about taking stuff back? Is that something you can do?"

"Why? Looking to send a postcard to your mum?"

"Not exactly," said Harold, "But what about letters and things like that? Is that something you're able to do?" This seemed to anger the captain, who rose from his seat and made his way to the window. He wasn't a tall man, but was well-built, and could easily be older than he looked. Harold had always heard how sailors looked older than they were and figured it was because of the constant wind and seawater they faced.

"I come here offering you a service, sticking my neck out for someone I barely know, and you want me to go further out of my way still? The audacity!" His voice was deep and husky, like a heavy smoker after years of chain-smoking. Harold scrambled to think of a way to get the captain back on his side.

"I don't have much, but I'll find a way to pay you for your efforts." At this, the captain made his way over to Harold, who was still sat on his bed. He didn't think the captain would go searching through his bed sheets for secretive letters, but Harold wanted to make sure. The captain's short stature meant he was almost eye-level with Harold, even though he was sitting down. The angered look on the captain's weathered face soon turned to a wicked smile, and he let out a small, almost faked laugh.

"A man after my own heart, you are, Mr. Kobbs. Taking items back to the mainland is more difficult than bringing things in, but I'll see what I can do." Harold wasn't sure what it was, but something made him trust the boat captain. He had an aura around him that the residents didn't, almost as if he wasn't one of them. The captain offered a hand to Harold, who responded with a handshake. "Call me Cal," said the captain, "I try to come ashore maybe once a week, but sometimes it's less than that. I'll make sure to come and find you when I'm back next unless you've got something you want me to take now?"

"Next time sounds good," said Harold with a smile.

Cal nodded and made his way back into the hallway, taking another swig from his flask as he closed the wooden door of Harold's room. With this new opportunity having presented itself, Harold immediately made his way to where the captain had sat and began writing a letter to Maria. Harold's handwriting had never been particularly good, but he tried his best to make it eligible for her to read. After several attempts that were scrapped after just a few words, he sat back in his chair, puzzled as to how he could begin a letter of such magnitude. He finally settled on *'Maria, I'm sorry. Please allow me to explain my actions'*.

By the time Harold had written a letter he was happy with, it had grown dark outside. Stroking the stubble that had formed along his jawline, he still couldn't decide if he should read Yvette's letter tonight, or in the morning. Either way, he wouldn't be sleeping well tonight.

Finally deciding on reading it before he slept, Harold placed the chair in front of his door for extra insurance against anyone barging their way in, took the letter out from under the bedsheets, and opened the envelope. It had been bent up and looked like it had been read several times. Then Harold remembered the state of Yvette's room, and thought perhaps it was like that before she'd even written it.

To Manu,

I'm writing this hoping that it won't be my last chance to speak to you but anticipating that it might be. I've found some kind of factory out in the woods past Jerry's. I don't know what it's there for, but it's definitely being used. There were people outside, the lights were on, and it sounded like there were machines inside. I'm going to go back there tonight.

If you don't hear from me again, look after Franziska, and for god's sake, get together.

Thank you for being a good friend, but I'll never forgive you for that cheap move you pulled at chess a few years ago. I hope you take that to the grave with you, you bastard.

-   Yvette.
-

Harold was concerned that this letter was seemingly the last anyone had heard from Yvette. As he placed the letter back into the envelope, he laid his head down and closed his eyes, wondering if he'd do better preparing himself for what the factory had in store, rather than rushing in head-first.

The following morning Harold woke to the same smell of cooked meat that had awoken him two days before. Peering through the small window of his room, Harold was somewhat relieved to see the chicken roll stall was once again set up, and that the smell wasn't emanating from within his room. Mrs. Sands was handing out chicken rolls to the passing residents, whilst tending to the grill behind her every chance she got.

Outside, Harold was met by the sound of seagulls calling, undoubtedly trying to get their share of Mrs. Sands' chicken rolls. Debating whether or not to indulge in another bland roll, Harold rubbed his cheeks with his hands, feeling the prickly stubble beneath his fingers. Across the market he spotted Charlie, with his signature large afro, helping two residents Harold hadn't seen before: two ladies, almost the polar opposite of each other. One was large in both height and build, whilst the other seemed small and slim. Whilst the larger lady had a thick mop of hair that fell to her shoulders, the smaller one had hair shorter than Harold's, slicked back with gel. Harold wondered if the two were related, as their similar facial features and matching ginger hair would suggest so.

By now, Harold's stomach began to rumble, and against his better judgement, he decided to give the chicken rolls another try. Thanking Mrs. Sands as she handed over the food wrapped in a paper towel, Harold heard what sounded like someone trying to get his attention from the path to the docks. He noticed Christian leaning against the wall of one of the buildings that towered over the path, licking his fingertips. He tilted his head back in a sharp motion, gesturing for Harold to make his way over.

Christian was dressed in a green sweater, with the shirt sleeves rolled up, revealing several scars running up his arms. Even being somewhat dressed down, he still managed to make the outfit look formal.

"Good morning, Mr. Kobbs. Decided to give the chicken rolls another go?"

"I'll be honest, more through necessity than desire," replied Harold, proud at himself for creating such an elegant sounding sentence on the fly.

"Please, will you join me?" Christian gestured down the path towards the docks, and the two began to walk. "You know, this place is full of secrets," continued Christian, whilst Harold took a bite of his food. "It has to be. I mean, look at the people around you. Misfits, criminals, people that society has deemed 'bad'. Secrets are the foundation of this island. Everybody has them, everybody knows that their neighbours and friends here have them, and, for the most part, everybody keeps them to themselves. But I will share one with you now, Harold."

As they reached the docks, Christian stopped, looking out to sea. The fog made it hard to tell what the sea was like further out, but from what Harold could see, it was mostly calm. The light waves that crashed against the rocks of the island kicked up a small amount of foam, the smell of which overpowered the scent of Harold's food. "That's not chicken you're eating, Harold," said Christian, continuing to look out towards the emptiness. With an eyebrow raised, Harold lowered the roll from his mouth, small parts of it stuck between his teeth.

"Then what is it?" he asked. Christian turned to face him, a friendly smile now donning the thick lips of the smartly dressed man.

"It's pork," said Christian, "schnitzel, to be exact. Franzi taught Mrs. Sands how to make it. When it's breaded, like that," he pointed towards Harold's food, "it's almost indistinguishable from breaded chicken. Well, to those that don't know, I suppose."

"Schnitzel? Why?"

"Pork is a lot easier to come by for the captain than chicken," came the reply, "but some people are a bit uneasy about eating pork. Charlie, for example. Religious reasons or something."

"So, you're lying to everybody?"

"Harold," Christian placed his hand on Harold's shoulder, "I never asked for this. I never wanted to be in charge of an island of misfits. But, sometimes, life just thrusts things upon you, and that's how leaders are made. You either rise to the occasion, or you become another sheep. Not that there's anything wrong with sheep, of course, they're also tasty."

Christian removed his hand from Harold's shoulder before taking a seat on the edge of the docks. He threw his thin legs over the side, his feet tentatively touching the foam laying on top of the water below. "When I came here, I was just a child." Christian's whole demeanor changed, from what seemed like a happy and confident man, to one much more sombre and honest. "My father brought me here, I must have been about 5 or 6? Old enough to know what was going on, but not old enough to see the bigger picture. He told me that we were moving away from my mother, that she didn't love us anymore, and wanted us to go." Christian was staring deeply into the sea, speaking as if he just wanted to get something off his chest, rather than directly to Harold. "Of course, I later learned that this was a lie, and he just wanted to be spiteful and take me away from her as some sick act of revenge. But, by the time I realised this, it was too late."

Harold was unsure if it would seem rude to finish his roll whilst Christian spoke about something that clearly upset him. He wasn't sure why Christian had decided to confess this to him, or if it was even true. The stress lines that had now formed on Christian's head, however, lead Harold to believe that he was, in fact, telling the truth. Harold took a seat next to Christian, placing a hand on his shoulder as Christian had done to him, and put the half-eaten roll down on the warped wood of the dock between them.

"Did you ever speak to her again?" asked Harold, trying to get Christian to look at him.

"Never," replied Christian, still looking into the sea beneath his feet, "I heard that she died, but not before re-marrying. Had kids too, I heard. Moved on from my father and me pretty quickly, she did. But, from what I remember of her, she was an honest and kind woman, much better than my father deserved. So, if that's what helped her cope, then I don't blame her. We all have our little comforts, I suppose."

"Exactly," said Harold, in the hope of cheering him up. He could see that Christian cracked a small smile once again, but was now looking along the coast of the island that curved into the fog ahead.

"It's strange, those little comforts we have. My mother needed a new family, but all you needed was Kraftwerk." Harold laughed, looking down at his half-eaten roll.

"You can't judge me for that, your comfort is a chicken roll that's not even chicken." The two laughed, and Christian finally made eye contact with Harold again. Harold tore the remainder of the roll in half, offering some to Christian which he gladly accepted. "Besides, if you've never listened to *The Man Machine*, you're missing out."

"Prove it," said Christian, sharply. "I've got a record player in my office. Grab the record, and you can introduce me to the world that is Kraftwerk." Harold nodded and began to make his way back to the square. "Meet me by the fountain in 10," called Christian from the docks.

It wasn't until Harold was back in the cramped space he called his room that he had remembered Yvette's letter and the factory she spoke of. Christian's talk of secrets on the island made him question if Christian knew of the factory, or if he'd played any part in what had happened to Yvette and Jerry. It was a bit of a stretch at this point, as Harold had no proof of a solid connection, but at the very least it was suspect. Deciding not to mention anything about the missing pair just yet, Harold grabbed the vinyl from his room and made his way back to the square.

Sat against the concrete bowl of the fountain was Christian, along with the two red-headed girls he'd seen Charlie helping earlier that morning.

"Harold! Meet Gill and Daisy, they'll be joining us for our Kraftwerk listening party."

"Hello," replied Harold, caught slightly off guard by the brief introduction. "How are you?"

"No time for that now, Harold!" said Christian, taking a step away from the fountain. "Come, to my office. I'll introduce everybody properly there." Christian placed his arm around Harold like an old friend and walked briskly onwards.

Making their way past the red brick building Harold was staying in, the group climbed a set of stone steps Harold hadn't noticed before and wondered how many other routes away from the square he hadn't yet seen. As they continued past more small houses,

Christian pointed to the distance, where the stub of a lighthouse came into view through the fog. Christian explained how, many years ago, a huge storm had knocked the top part of the lighthouse into the sea, and how he'd salvaged the remaining structure by fashioning it into a home for himself. As the group continued down the path, the small brick buildings were replaced by what looked like carefully planted trees, turning the path into a showpiece of a walkway that curved round to the lighthouse. Surrounding the base of the lighthouse was a kind of housing complex, consisting of several one-storey buildings. Christian took a step ahead of the group and welcomed them with his arms outstretched. "My friends, welcome to Wile Manor. It's not much, but it's home."

Christian took the group into one of the smaller buildings at the base of the lighthouse, where the inside consisted of a pub-like setup, much like the ground floor of the red brick building. The only difference here was that there were fewer chairs and more sofas. The bar sat almost identical to the one in the red brick building, and soon Christian was behind it, making drinks for the group. Gesturing Harold over to the record player, Harold took the record out of its sleeve, and placed it down.

For the next few hours, the group listened to the vinyl's electronic and futuristic sounds, frequently topping up their drinks and changing seats. Harold was a little disappointed that the girls didn't seem to enjoy the record as much as he did, but he made the effort to talk to them and get to know them. Although they were sisters, they'd come to the island some time apart and were the first siblings to have settled on Galkirk since Christian had taken charge. Although he wasn't a smoker, Harold joined Gill on her occasional smoke breaks, which Christian requested they took over by the door.

By the time Harold plucked up the courage to ask Christian more about the island, they were both several drinks in, which Harold hoped would work to his advantage. As Harold made his way over to Christian, the click of the metronome kicked in, followed by an isolated sound of electronic keys on loop. Kraftwerk's titular track of the album, *The Man Machine*, began to play.

"Christian, you said you never wanted to be in charge of the island? Can I ask what happened?" By now, Christian's eyelids hung heavily over his eyes and he looked as though he was struggling to stay awake.

"You can ask," he slurred, "but that doesn't mean I'll answer."

"What about your dad?" asked Harold, trying his luck once again.

"What about him?"

"What happened to him?"

"Harold, Harold, Harold," said Christian, "You're not very good at this whole 'not asking questions' thing, are you? It's going to get you in trouble one day," said Christian in a light-hearted way.

By now, Gill and Daisy were asleep on one of the sofas opposite Harold and Christian. As Christian checked his watch for the time, Harold got a better look at the scars on his arms. Now that he was closer, he could see that Christian's thin arms were full of scars, ranging from small and faded marks to thick lines a few inches long. The only exception was a small, square-shaped scar about halfway up his left arm, as if a patch of skin had been damaged or cut. None of the scars seemed fresh; they all looked to have healed some time ago. Harold noticed that, strangely, none of the scars reached past his wrists and his hands were completely scar-free.

"Goodness, look at the time!" Christian was still slurring his words, and as he hauled himself upright, he clapped his hands to wake up the sisters. "It's time for bed, everyone. As much as I'd like you all to stay, I know you've got homes to go to. Please be safe." The girls stumbled over to the door, rubbing their eyes as they did, whilst Christian once again placed his arm over Harold and walked him outside. The cold night air engulfed Harold from head to toe, causing him to shiver as soon as he stepped outside.

"Christian, at least tell me one thing. What are all of these buildings for if it's just you who lives here?" Harold was determined not to let the night go to waste, and although he'd undoubtedly hit up some kind of friendship with the strange and charismatic Christian, he still hoped to see more of the vulnerable and talkative man he'd spoken to on the docks that morning.

"Chess, my friend, Chess and mysteries." came the reply, with Christian's arm still laying over Harold's firm shoulders "There's two things my dad told me that I'll remember forever. The first is that life is a game of chess – you should always plan at least two steps ahead of your opponent."

"And the second?"

"Not all mystery's need solving." Christian removed his arm from Harold's shoulder and patted him on the back as a goodbye.

Harold stumbled his way back to his room, feeling that, although he'd enjoyed his time with Christian and the sisters, he'd wasted valuable time in finding answers to where Jerry and Yvette had gone. Apart from Gill and Daisy, whom he'd walked back to the square with, Harold hadn't seen anybody around the town, which was no surprise considering the time of night. He fumbled his way up the stairs of the red brick building and threw himself into bed, his head spinning with a mixture of alcohol-based confusion and questions.

Christian had watched the three stumble and sway up the path away from his complex until they merged into the fog and disappeared. As soon as the visitors were out of sight, he snapped out of his drunken act and stood himself upright. He made his way back into the bar area to put away both the whisky he'd been serving his guests, and the apple juice he'd been pretending was alcohol for himself. He removed the needle from Harold's vinyl that he'd left behind and placed the record back into its sleeve. "What absolute drivel," he said to himself, whilst studying the artwork.

He made his way outside and placed his key into the padlock on one of the buildings surrounding the base of the lighthouse. With one firm turn, the padlock snapped open and dropped to the floor. Christian pulled open the stiff wooden door to the single room building and felt for the light switch inside. The stench was horrendous, making Christian's nostrils to flair uncontrollably. He found the light switch and flicked it up, causing a single lightbulb to flicker and stutter before finally dimly lighting the room. Sat in the centre, chained down in the wheelchair he sat in, was a frail old man. His long, grey hair was thin and greasy, and the old man's fingernails extended far past his fingertips. His eyes were a milky white and didn't react at all to the light that hung directly above him. Christian wondered if the old man was still alive, and removed his oxygen mask to check. His dry, cracked lips parted slightly, revealing a small set of yellowed and brown stained teeth. He let out a small groan, his eyes still not moving, as if he hadn't seen Christian stood in front of him.

"Well, you certainly had me there, old man, I thought you were a goner. Anyway, not to worry, it's dinner time." Christian made his way to a small refrigerator that sat in the far corner of the room and removed a small lump of uncooked meat from within. "I know this isn't exactly the retirement you dreamed of, Dad, but you're lucky I'm even looking after you, all things considered."

Chapter 7:
Relations.

Harold struggled to pull himself up out of bed the next morning. His head was thumping, no doubt from the copious amounts of alcohol from the night before. Checking his watch, which he'd forgotten to remove before getting into bed, he realised he'd already slept longer than he'd wanted. Studying the gold rim of the watch's face, he remembered the day Maria had bought it for him.

It had been Harold's 30th birthday, and they'd travelled to Covent Garden for the day, with Maria promising to buy Harold anything he wanted. Harold had never been particularly interested in watches but had fallen in love with one as soon as he saw it in the shop window – the same way he'd felt the moment he first saw Maria. It was fairly plain and not especially big, but its simplicity was what Harold liked. Expecting it to cost more, Maria had surprised Harold by also buying him Kraftwerk's *Autobahn* whilst they browsed a record store. That day was one of Harold's favourite memories. As he wondered what Maria would be doing now, Harold squeezed his eyes shut in the hope of holding back the tears, but this only hurt his head more. Deciding he needed some fresh air, he quickly showered in the shared bathroom and made his way downstairs.

To Harold's surprise, the bar area of the red brick building was filled with people. It was still morning, but residents crowded the bar, trying to grab the attention of the poor soul tending to it. As Harold tried to make sense of what was happening, he saw several of the residents make their way into the rain outside. Spotting the large stature of his neighbour Charlie, Harold called to him hoping to get answers, but the tall man didn't notice. Chasing after him into the rain, Harold called to him once again, this time managing to grab his attention and ask him what was happening. He explained that Harold had missed a meeting where Christian had informed the residents of two new arrivals. One was expected in the next hour or so, and the second would be later that day.

"Why didn't you wake me?" asked Harold, angrily.

"I tried!" said Charlie, "I knocked a few times, but I thought you weren't in."

Harold suspected Charlie of lying, but he looked sincere, leading Harold to wonder if he'd been so deeply asleep that he hadn't heard Charlie knocking.

Harold began to think this would be a good time to investigate the factory Yvette had written about, but he had some doubts. He wasn't nearly friendly enough with any of the residents to have them cover for him yet, so if he did meet the same fate as Jerry and Yvette, he would be gone; not just to Maria and the outside world, but for real.

Looking around for a familiar face, Harold saw the twins from the night before, but there was no sign of Christian, Manu, or Franziska. Fearing the worst, Harold made his way up to Manu's room. He knocked once on Manu's door as hard as he could, but immediately regretted his decision. Clenching his hand into a fist sent shooting pains through his arm, causing his shoulder to drop slightly. Looking down, he could see that his hand was shaking uncontrollably. The yellow and purple discolouration still decorated the area around his knuckle, and he began to wonder if he'd done more damage than just severe bruising and dislocation.

As Harold stood cradling his bad hand, Manu emerged from his room. His hair was pulled back into the two buns that he was known for, and a thin cigarette hung loosely from his lips. Wearing only a small pair of Y-fronts, the Italian seemed to have no shame in answering the door in his underwear.

"Little man," said the Italian through pursed lips, "what's wrong? You look stressed." Manu invited Harold in and offered him the seat at his desk, which he kindly refused. Sat upright in Manu's bed was Franziska, also smoking a cigarette, with the bedsheets barely covering her breasts. Noticing this, Harold tried his best to avoid looking but doing so made his attempts all the more obvious in the process.

"I- uh, just wanted to make sure you were both OK," said Harold, his eyes darting around, looking at all four corners of the ceiling. "There was a meeting about some new residents, but I didn't see you there." Noticing Harold's discomfort, Manu threw a shirt over to Franziska that she pulled over her head. Showing his thanks with a smile, Harold dropped his over the top theatrics.

"How's the record?" Asked Franziska, smiling at Harold. He continued to avoid eye-contact with her, nodding his head to tell her it was good. At this point, Harold realised he'd left the record at Christian's place, and made a mental note to retrieve it later.

"We were taking stock," said Manu, winking at Franziska, and the two shared a laugh. "Which reminds me, have you found yourself a job yet, little man?"

"No," replied Harold, "why?"

"I need help with some of the stock coming in today. Fancy earning yourself a few tokens?"

Harold agreed, hoping that spending time with Manu would help him strike up some kind of friendship, and maybe open Manu up to talking a bit more about Yvette. Manu asked him to meet him by the docks in an hour, saying he needed to "finish things up first".

By the time Harold finally spotted Manu through the fog, he was nearly half an hour late. Manu blamed his lateness on 'admin errors', which Harold decided not to think too much about. The two talked shop for a bit, with Manu explaining that the captain was bringing in a shipment of second-hand hats that Harold and Manu would have to sort through to sell at the market. As Manu began to describe the process of figuring out the sizes, the two were interrupted by the distant roar of the boat's engines. Slowly, the outline of the boat began to emerge through the fog, bobbing side to side as it rode the waves towards the docks. The rain was still in the air but had eased into a drizzle.

Harold could see the captain readying the ship for its arrival, preparing the rope as he had done when Harold had first come to the island. As Harold began to wave at the captain through the fog, a voice came from behind him.

"You shouldn't distract a sailor when he's hard at work, my friend." It was Christian, dressed as he had been when Harold had arrived. Smiling at the two, he made his way next to them, creating the sort of welcome party Harold had expected to receive.

"I hope you've asked the captain to bring some salad with him, Christian," said Manu as he lit up a cigarette.

"Salad?" Christian looked deeply confused, his eyebrow raised and his eyes wide.

"He's one of those people who don't eat meat, can't remember if he's veggie or vegan. The captain was telling me the other day."

"Is he now?" Christian's expression changed from confusion to deep thought, as if all the cogs in his head were turning at once. "How interesting."

As the boat arrived, a young man with a thick mop of blonde hair emerged from the cabin. Dressed head to toe in a tweed suit, he carried with him two large suitcases. Harold noticed that, despite his young age, every one of his possessions looked expensive. His suit matched Christian's in terms of elegance, and the suitcases looked like the type you'd find without price tags on – indicating that they were costly. Before Harold could offer his help, Christian stepped forward, introducing himself.

"Ewan, if I'm not mistaken? Please, let me take one of those." Christian took one of the suitcases from the young man, as he stepped off the boat and onto the docks.

"Over there are Harold and Manu, you'll meet them properly later. However, we've much to discuss. So, please, follow me." Christian lead the young man up the path past Harold and Manu. As they passed, Ewan began to stare at Harold, with a puzzled look on his face. Harold stared back until the young man and Christian disappeared between the two buildings that stood either side of the path.

Manu climbed aboard the boat and began passing crates to Harold. The captain was already preparing to disembark, but gave Harold a nod as if to reiterate what he'd said the day before. Harold returned the nod before Manu jumped back to the dock, took a crate from the pile Harold was holding and made his way back to the square. As Harold followed him, he heard the roar of the boat engine once again and wondered how hard it would be to sneak aboard and return to the mainland.

When the two arrived back at Manu's room, they began to open the crates and sort through the hats inside. Ranging from caps and beanies to large-brimmed wedding hats, there seemed to be no rhyme or reason to the crate's contents. It was as if someone had raided a charity shop for every hat in stock and sent them to the island. Harold asked Manu where exactly the hats had come from, but his answer was unconvincing and vague.

A few hours passed, and as they finished attaching price tags to the hats, Harold checked his watch again. It was now 6 PM, and apart from the packet of nuts Manu had given him, Harold hadn't eaten all day. Peering through the window in the hope of spotting Mrs. Sands' stall, he was disappointed to see that the square was empty. Manu explained that Mrs. Sands' had no set days of trade, other than market days. When she had stock, she'd set up and begin serving, but they'd been lucky that she had been set up regularly the past few days. When the two had attached the final price tags, Manu gave Harold the blue strip of paper marked with 6 tokens, as well as half a loaf of bread, and a block of cheese.

"Call it a 'thank you' for all your hard work today, and *not* for keeping quiet about Franzi and me." Manu winked at Harold, and he understood. He put the blue strip into his pocket, thanked Manu, and began to make his way back to his room, all the while thinking about the best way to find the factory tonight.

Out in the square stood the new resident, Ewan, still dressed in his tweed suit, looking up at the buildings around him. As Harold tried to pass him, he extended his arm, stopping Harold in his tracks.

"I know you," said Ewan, still looking up at the buildings above them. Turning his head to get a better look, Harold could see that, even if this man *did* know who he was, Harold didn't know him. Keeping his guard up, Harold asked how the man knew him. "That's what I'm trying to work out." Ewan stopped looking at the buildings and instead focused on Harold, looking him up and down. From his behaviour, Harold could tell that Galkirk's newest resident thought he was cock of the walk and wondered how long that'd fly with Christian.

Harold tilted his head to the side, as he often would when he felt as though he was in trouble. Slowly clenching his fist, careful not to cause the same pain he had when he'd knocked on Manu's door, he was ready for whatever the young man could throw at him. Yet, just as Harold could feel his body tensing up, Ewan lowered his arm.

"Ah, it'll come to me. But I definitely know you."

Harold chose to ignore his remark and continued towards the red brick building. However, before he reached the large wooden doors, they opened outward, and Christian emerged from inside. As he went to greet Harold, the young man started again.

"I've got it! I saw you in the paper! You tried to kill her lover or something?"

Harold's shoulders dropped. Somehow, hearing somebody say it out loud caused the memory to come flooding back to him. The blood, the sound of bone crashing against the concrete, Maria's scream, everything. It overwhelmed him, causing him to shake and quiver in fear of what he'd done. This was the first time he'd heard it said aloud, and it crippled him.

Seeing what Ewan's words had done to him, Christian offered a hand to Harold, who was now crouched on the floor, holding open hands in front of his face. Even though his eyes were wide, Harold couldn't see Christian's hand in front of him. He couldn't see anything, except for the memory of what he'd done, replaying over and over again in his head.

"Don't worry, friend, I've got you," said Christian, as he brought Harold back to his feet. "I brought your Kraftwerk album back, slid it under your door. Go sit down, relax. It's OK." With a pat on Harold's back, Christian made his way towards Ewan. As Harold stumbled his way to the large wooden doors of the red brick building, he heard Christian from behind him say: "Ewan, we need to speak about a few things. First of all, I hear you don't eat meat?"

Fumbling his way up to his room, Harold began to regain a sense of clarity. Reassuring himself that he'd acted in self-defence, his mind started to clear by the time he'd closed the door of his room behind him. Careful not to step on the vinyl Christian had slid under his door, Harold picked it up and placed it onto the record player he'd found at Jerry's. The sound of the drum machines on loop began to soothe Harold, and soon he found himself sprawled out on his bed. He closed his eyes, visualising the sounds of the synthesisers and keyboard as shapes and colours. The visual Harold could see when he closed his eyes and listened to Kraftwerk reminded him of when he was a child, and he used to rub his eyes so much that he'd see shapes and colours when he closed them.

Woken by the sound of knocking, Harold wasn't aware that he'd even fallen asleep. Three sharp knocks came from behind the door once again. As he opened it, Christian stood leaning on the doorway, his suit a different colour from the one he'd been wearing earlier. Harold invited him into the room and Christian unfastened the last button on his waistcoat before sitting down.

"Do you want to talk about what happened in the square?" asked Christian. His voice was low and soft, as if he was trying not to startle Harold. He sat back in the chair, his hands perched upon his knees, and breathed deeply. "He knows you, doesn't he? He was right about what he saw in the paper?" Harold was sat on his bed, facing Christian, and he nodded in response.

"Hearing it said out loud by a stranger like that, I don't know what happened. It just hit me like a ton of bricks."

"It looked like you went into shock, Harold."

"I don't know why I did it," said Harold. Christian inhaled, ready to dish out some advice for Harold, but soon noticed that he hadn't finished speaking, so allowed Harold to continue. "I could see it in her eyes. I knew what they'd been doing behind my back." Harold's eyes began to twitch from left to right as he stared into the carpet beneath him. "Then, one day, he had the audacity to come to my house. I saw the way he was looking at Maria. I knew. He was getting some kind of sick thrill out of it." Harold's breathing became erratic, and his eyes began to widen once again.

"And then what?" asked Christian, still sitting calmly on the chair in front of Harold.

"I- I just," Harold closed his eyes, thinking back to what had happened. "Something happened inside my head. Like, I reached a boiling point. I just snapped."

"Harold, tell me. What exactly did you do?"

"I went for him. I started with the eyes. I tried to push my thumbs into his eyes, but I only made contact with my left thumb. I didn't realise that my right was pressing onto the bone of his eye socket, and my knuckle popped out."

"Harold, that's brutal." Despite what Christian had to say, his voice remained calm and collected, and he spoke as if he wanted Harold to continue.

"Well, yes. But you don't understand, Christian, the rage I felt towards this man was unbearable. I've never fought anyone in my life, and I didn't know what to do. But I wanted him gone. In that moment, I just wanted him to disappear. I pushed him to the ground, his head hit the pavement, and it was the most horrendous sound I've ever heard." Harold raised his palms to his eyes, as he began to feel the tears forming. He tried his hardest to hold them back, and soon felt Christian's hands on his shoulders once again.

"Harold, Galkirk is a place to escape all of that. I know you're a good person at heart, and I know that what you did was a freak lapse of personality. What you did doesn't make you a bad person." Christian's advice didn't seem to help, as Harold continued to cover his eyes with his hands. Trying once again to comfort Harold, Christian tried a different approach. "I'll sort out the new boy, don't worry." He made his way over to the door but paused before opening it. "Take as much time as you need, Harold. I want you to feel as comfortable as possible here. And if that means taking some time for yourself, that's fine. If you need to talk, I'll be at my place. I'll even let you bring your record again if it helps."

"Thank you," Harold managed to muster from behind his hands.

Harold heard Christian making his way downstairs, and as the sound of footsteps stopped, he shot up from his bed and looked out of the window. He watched until Christian had made his way up the path towards the lighthouse, before grabbing a coat, Yvette's diary, and a pen. Wiping the tears from his eyes, he darted down the stairs and out into the square. He pulled his hood up to protect himself from the rain, stuffed the diary and pen into his pocket, and sprinted towards Jerry's shop.

Harold slipped on the wet cobblestone underfoot as he approached his old friend's shop. Peering inside, he could see that nothing had changed since Jerry had disappeared. He tried the door, but it didn't budge. Looking down, he saw a thick brass padlock now prevented anybody from entering the shop. Harold pulled out the diary and pen, scrawled in a quick entry about the padlock, and stuffed them back into the coat pocket, continuing down the bath described in both Yvette's diary and letter to Manu.

By the time Harold reached the end of the path, the rain was torrential. He couldn't see much of what was ahead, but he noticed a slightly worn patch of grass leading away from the edge of the cobblestone and assumed that it was the same route Yvette had spoken about. Pushing back all manner of branches and leaves, Harold began to hear a distant rumbling coming from somewhere ahead of him. The sun was setting, and it would soon be dark, so Harold decided to pick up the pace and continue along the poor excuse of a path towards the noise. At one point, a small branch whipped Harold on his right cheek, cutting him. It wasn't deep, but it stung, and the rain that continued to hit him in the face only caused him more discomfort.

Soon enough, Harold found himself approaching a clearing from the trees, and he could see the factory Yvette had written about. He now understood why Yvette had been so fascinated with it, as it seemed very out of place for somewhere as quiet and sleepy as Galkirk. Placing the diary in some light that was emitting from the factory, Harold scribbled down another quick entry, before looking towards the factory for any sign of life. Sure enough, at one end, he could see several people dressed in blue aprons, stood in a circle and having a smoke. Wiping away the rain that was dripping from his eyebrow, Harold tried to count how many people he could see.

He decided on either five or six, but the distance and the rain were making it difficult to be exact. As Harold decided what to do next, the horrific sound coming from the factory came to an abrupt stop with lights from within soon following suit. His eyes began to adapt to the lack of light and before long he saw the figures in blue aprons, of which there now seemed to be more than five or six, walking away from the factory. Whatever they'd been doing, they'd now finished.

Making his way gingerly through the woodland, Harold began to follow the group. He lost sight of them every so often through the trees and branches, only to find them again a few seconds later. Luckily, the rain would likely mask the sound of his footsteps, but he kept his distance just in case. As Harold watched the group of now around nine or ten approaching a crossroad, he expected them to turn right towards the square. However, to his surprise, they all turned left, moving further away from the square and deeper into the woods. Harold tried to scribble a third entry in Yvette's diary, but the light was now too poor and the rain too heavy. He debated going back to the square to find Manu and tell him that what Yvette said in the letter had been true all along, but Harold's curiosity was peaking once again, and adrenaline was coursing through his veins. What was inside the factory? Where was the group going? He couldn't let his questions go unanswered any longer. He shoved the diary back into his coat pocket and continued to follow the group into the forest.

Chapter 8:
Discoveries.

The mud was beginning to stick to Harold's shoes, making his feet feel heavy and cumbersome. He'd been following the group of strangers through the forest for at least half an hour, but as they carried on down the path away from the square, Harold couldn't help but feel like he'd made the wrong choice. The rain was lashing down, smacking him in the face every time the wind kicked up. Water was dripping heavily from his eyebrows and nose at this point, and he was wiping off the excess any time he wasn't pushing stray branches out of his way.

The rain was the heaviest he'd seen since arriving on Galkirk, and in the back of his mind he hoped the second newcomer Christian spoke of arrived safely. If he made it out of this investigation alive, Harold planned on becoming friendly with the new resident, hoping to make an ally to help find his missing friend – assuming they weren't like Ewan.

Harold followed the group for a while longer, and soon they came to another opening in the forest. Taking cover behind a large fallen tree, Harold took a closer look at what was in the clearing. Dimly lit by hanging lamps was what seemed like another small town, only this time the buildings looked different. They looked less like the buildings that surrounded the square, and more like the ones Christian had built around the base of the lighthouse. They were all single-storey and had no outside decoration. Harold watched as the group disbanded and made their way into separate buildings, one of them entering the structure closest to Harold.

Looking for shelter, Harold noticed a small shed between the woods and the closest building. It wouldn't offer much protection but would be safer than sitting out in the rain all night. With no specific plan in mind, Harold crouched down low and made his way over to the shed. Trying the small wooden door, Harold was relieved when it opened without a fuss, and he stepped inside.

The dim light from the lamps outside broke through the wooden panels of the shed, revealing a small pile of plastic sheets in the centre. On the wall hung several large knives and other tools, as well as two blue aprons he'd seen the strangers wearing. Assessing his situation and the options available, Harold formulated a simple plan. He'd spend the night in the shed, and in the morning, he'd wear a blue apron to make his way back to the square. He wanted to investigate this strange new place, but he thought for sure someone would notice that they hadn't seen him there before. This way, he'd get a quick look at the place before returning for backup. He wasn't sure what exactly he'd do when he returned to the square, or who he'd talk to, but it was the only plan he had. Harold scribbled a few notes into Yvette's diary, describing what he'd seen, before hiding under the plastic sheets for the night.

Surprisingly, Harold slept well. The rain must have stopped shortly after he had entered the shed, as he slept right through the night without any disturbances. Checking his watch, he could see it was nearly 8 am, and it was time to get moving. Slipping the blue apron over his head, he psyched himself up for what was to come by slapping his cheeks. Immediately regretting his decision due to the cut on one cheek, and the bruise around his eye on the other side, he resorted to rubbing his cheeks instead, before inhaling deeply and stepping outside.

Harold froze. Almost immediately, he was met by a well-built figure with a shaved head, tattoos stretching from the side of their neck and over the top of their head. They were pushing some kind of cart but had been walking in front of the shed the moment Harold had stepped outside. The figure froze, looking at Harold. In a moment of madness, Harold panicked, figuring these would be his last breaths.

"Morning," he mustered.

"Morning, dude. Sleep well?" said the stranger. Their voice was deep, but looking closer at the stranger, Harold noticed that the intimidating figure was a woman. A muscular, intimidating, and terrifying woman.

"Yes. Fine. And you?" Harold thought for sure his race was run but decided to keep up the niceties on the off chance that he'd make it out of the encounter alive.

"Eh, so so. I knew I was stuck with cleaning out the shitters this morning. So, you know, not great." The stranger laughed, and Harold responded with laughter of his own. Fake and nervous laughter, but laughter all the same. "Anyway, best get to it. Have a good one!" said the stranger as she pushed the cart down past the buildings.

Still shocked at the pleasantness of the encounter, Harold stood still for a moment. Wondering if he'd dreamt the whole thing, he patted himself from his head down to his waist. Why had the woman not noticed that they'd never met before? Harold decided not to dwell on it too much, at least not whilst stood in a potentially dangerous place. As he made his way back towards the path he'd followed the strangers down the night before, he took a brief look in the direction the woman had gone. It looked just like a regular small town, with people strolling about, tending to their daily duties. The only difference Harold could see was that most, if not all, of the people here had tattoos on show – something he hadn't seen on the people in and around the square, and none of them were wearing the blue aprons he'd seen from previous night. Harold put his head down and made his way up the path towards the factory, and then to the square, tossing the apron into the woods when he was out of sight.

By the time Harold arrived back on the path by Jerry's shop, it was nearly 9 am. Passing his friend's shop, Harold saw Franziska sitting on the fountain, smoking a cigarette. Harold asked how she was and if she'd seen Manu, to which she told him he was still asleep. Harold made his way up to Manu's room and knocked three times, careful not to hurt his hand again. Answering the door in his Y-fronts for a second time, Manu yawned in Harold's face, characteristically unashamed that his almost naked body was on show.

"Little man, what is it? You're beginning to make a habit of seeing me in these, no?" He gestured towards his underwear, but Harold ignored him, barging past the Italian, and making his way into the room. "Harold, my friend, you stink! What on earth have you been doing?"

"Yvette was right, Manu! The factory is real, and there's another town full of people!"

"Slow the fuck down, little man," said Manu as he scratched the front of his Y-fronts nonchalantly, "what are you talking about? And why are you stinking up my room?"

"In the letter Yvette wrote to you. The factory she mentioned, I found it. And there's a whole other community of people not far from it."

Harold described everything he'd seen, from the factory in operation, to the bald-headed woman he'd spoken to. Manu remained in his underwear throughout Harold's rant, hanging on his every word. When Harold had finished speaking the room stayed silent, as if Manu was waiting for the fantastical tale to continue.

"Take a shower," said the Italian, "I need to get Franzi. We need to speak about this properly.

"But she said she didn't wa-"

"I know what she said!" snapped Manu, "But this is different. She needs to know about this."

By the time Harold had showered, Franzi now sat with arms crossed on Manu's bed, looking both concerned and annoyed. Harold explained what he'd seen once again, and both Manu and Franzi listened to his every word. The three then discussed what would happen next, and how they should approach the situation going forward. Finally, they settled on keeping a low profile, and making tentative enquiries to find out if anybody else knew about the second town. Harold would work with Manu in the meantime so as not to arouse suspicion, and they'd discuss their findings in a few days' time.

The following days proved fruitless for Harold. Subtly mentioning how he wondered if there was space for another community on the island to Charlie, the twins, and Doctor Halter, all of them had claimed they either thought it was impossible, or that the island was too small. By the time the next market day came around, Harold realised he hadn't seen Ewan since his arrival, and hadn't seen the second newcomer at all.

Harold made his way into the market square early enough that the stalls were still being set up for the big day. The sky was the clearest it had been since Harold's arrival, and it was surprisingly warm for the time of year. With no sign of rain, Harold expected a successful day for the likes of Manu and Franziska. Making his way over to his Italian friend, Harold noticed he was speaking to a blonde woman he didn't think he'd seen before. As she turned towards, Harold knew he definitely hadn't seen her before, as he would have noticed her if he had. The delicate features of her face were almost perfectly symmetrical, and her hair was platinum blonde with brown highlights that sat in neat curls down to her shoulders. She gave Harold a shy smile as the two made eye contact, and Harold immediately felt butterflies in his stomach, like a schoolboy when his crush says hello to him. He hadn't felt this way since the first time he saw Maria many years ago, but the butterflies soon gave way to a sense of guilt as he remembered her. As the woman made her way around the market, Manu noticed Harold, and beckoned him over with a wave of his hand.

"My friend, she's a stunner, eh?" Manu raised an eyebrow and tilted his head towards the blonde-haired lady. "You should go and say hello!"

"I've already met the love of my life, Manu. And her name is Maria," said Harold, sombrely.

"Maria? No. I don't remember what she said her name was, but it definitely wasn't Maria."

"Back home, I mean."

"I know what you meant, little man. Still, she's lovely eh? She even told me she likes middle-aged men with black eyes and unkempt beards!" At this, Harold felt his cheeks once again. Feeling the bristle of his scruffy beard beneath his fingers reminded him of when he'd tried to grow it several years ago, but Maria had told him it wasn't a good look.

Harold asked Manu if he'd managed to get any more information on the second town, but the Italian had found nothing. For the next hour or so, as the market began to get busier, the two discussed their options going forward, keeping their voices as low as possible. Manu's stall was filled with new stock, most of which Harold recognised from when he and Manu had sorted the delivery. Harold noticed a black hat with a wide brim that he hadn't seen before and decided to try it on. It wasn't his usual style, and wasn't the sort of hat he'd have worn back home, but he took a strange liking to it, and it fit perfectly. Looking at himself in one of the small mirrors Manu had hanging from the roof of his stall, Harold asked how much it was.

"Usually, it'd cost 2 tokens, but if it's going to hide that ugly bruise on your face, call it half." Clipping the blue strip of paper, Manu smiled to himself, pleased with the joke he'd made.

Happy with his purchase, Harold strolled around the market, proud as a peacock. He tried to engage with Franziska to see if she'd learned anything, but she was busy talking to a few of the residents that were browsing her record collection. He hoped some of the inhabitants would compliment his new headwear, but nobody did. Not even Charlie, who Harold was sure looked directly at it, said anything when Harold greeted him.

Feeling a little deflated, Harold sat on a nearby bench, observing the residents enjoy their day of browsing the market. After a while of watching people of all shapes and sizes, somebody sat down next to him – the blonde lady. Panicking slightly, Harold tipped his new hat towards her, immediately regretting his decision. Before he could dwell too much on his strange introduction, she exhaled a sigh of what seemed like relief.

"What a strange place this is," she said, looking towards the market.

"Like you wouldn't believe," replied Harold, trying to keep his cool, "I'm Harold." He felt the butterflies in his stomach once again, but he did his best to remain calm.

"I know, Christian told me you're new here too?" As Harold mustered a response, he saw just how beautiful the blonde lady was. He felt as though he recognised her, and her eyes seemed familiar, although Harold couldn't place where he recognised her from. He nodded in response, and shuffled round to face Harold, looking him dead in the eye.

"And you know Jerry?" she asked, and Harold nodded once again. "This place isn't what you think it is, and if you haven't discovered it yet, you soon will." She slid a small piece of paper across the bench over to Harold, looking intensely into his eyes as she did. "Read this when nobody is looking and be careful who you trust." Before Harold could reply, she rose to her feet, adjusting her shirt as she did. "It was nice to meet you, Harold," she said in a loud voice, almost as if she wanted others to hear, "Thanks for the advice, I'll definitely try one of the chicken rolls." She made her way into the crowd of people around the market and disappeared from view.

Naturally, Harold ignored her instruction and read the note immediately. *The red brick building, room 9, tonight at 11pm. If you have a record player, bring it. Trust no one.* If she hadn't been so stern in the way she'd looked at him, he'd have thought this was some kind of flirty message, which Harold didn't mind. Once again ignoring her instructions, Harold made his way to tell Manu about the note.

"I knew it! The hat worked! Blonde lady wants a bit of the little man's little man, eh?" said Manu ecstatically. Harold shushed him, and eventually the Italian calmed down, telling Harold that he'd undercharged him for the hat.

Staring at his watch, impatiently waiting for 11 to approach, Harold's head began to spin. He wondered if the lady was some kind of undercover journalist, or if perhaps she was a private investigator who'd help him figure out the truth of what was happening. He imagined what would happen in the future, and how he'd somehow find a way to return home to Maria and continue his life from before. It was a long shot, but for a brief moment Harold believed it might happen, which made him smile.

Thinking back to the day's events, Harold realised that he hadn't seen Christian at the market. He'd returned to his room soon after receiving the note from the blonde lady, but Harold had expected to see Christian in some form during his time at the market. As he began to question where Christian had been, he noticed that the large hand of his watch had passed 11. He picked up his record player and began to make his way down the hall. He was sure he heard some movement downstairs as his made the short trip from his room to number 9, but by the time he shuffled the record player to one side to knock, the door opened. The blonde lady pulled Harold inside and bolted the door shut behind him.

"First things first, put the record player on. It'll help cover anything we say." As Harold stood clutching his record player, he was bemused by how different the blonde lady seemed from when she had smiled at him shyly just a few hours earlier. She stood by the door in a white tank top, revealing her toned arms and slim wrists. Harold caught himself staring, so decided to do as instructed, and set up the record player. He picked up the vinyl from the desk – something he didn't recognise - and placed it on the record player. As the wobbling voice of an opera singer began to fill the room, the blonde lady looked more relaxed. She took a seat on the bed, and Harold motioned to join her, but she quickly dismissed him, telling him to sit on the chair by the desk.

Before she could begin speaking, a knock came from behind the door. Her face turned to a scowl, directed at Harold as if to ask who had followed him. She gestured for him to hide against the wall, out of sight from anyone at the door, but as she gingerly pulled the door open, Harold recognised the voice immediately - it was Manu. He threw himself into the room with Franziska in tow, waving a hand at the blonde lady to close the door behind them.

"What the fuck are you two doing here?" She pointed a finger at Harold, who was still pinned against the wall, "Did you tell them?"

"He did," said Manu confidently, who had already made himself comfortable on the bed, "we're helping him to uncover the *mystery of Galkirk*," he continued, making quotation gestures with his hands.

"Even though we said we *weren't* getting involved," Franziska interjected, an air of annoyance in her voice. By now the blonde lady was ruffling her hair, as if she knew her control of the situation was already slipping.

"Harold," she said angrily, "should we expect any more guests?"

"Well, technically, I only told Manu. He must have told Franziska."

"Guilty," said Manu, raising his hands as if he'd been caught red-handed.

The blonde lady sighed, rubbing her eyes. She raised the palms of her hands towards the three guests in her room, taking control of the conversation.

"If we're all finished, I'd appreciate it if you all stayed quiet for a few minutes to let me explain what's going on." Seemingly with a change of heart, she directed Harold to join Manu and Franziska on her bed, whilst she took the seat he'd been sitting on. With all three sat upright facing her, she looked relaxed once again.

"My name is Sarah Jones. My dad, Jerry, is a resident here. I stopped receiving letters from him several days ago, so I'm here to find out what's happened to him." Harold snapped his fingers, realising that's how he recognised her eyes; they were the same as Jerry's. The others looked at Harold accusingly, wondering why, as it seemed to them, he'd just clicked his fingers for no reason.

"Wait a second," interrupted Manu, "how has he been sending letters to you? We're not supposed to have contact with people outside of the island?"

"The captain," said Harold under his breath, to which Sarah pointed in his direction. "The captain offered me the chance to take letters back to the mainland for me. That's how you've had contact with Jerry."

"Motherfucker! He didn't ask *me* if I wanted to send any letters!" Manu looked at Franziska, his eyes asking if she'd been given the same opportunity. Her avoidance of eye-contact confirmed that she had. Choosing to ignore the disruption, Sarah continued.

"He had been telling me about some of the residents disappearing, so as soon as his letters stopped, I made my way out here. Whatever is happening, I'm going to get to the bottom of it." Her focus turned to Harold, who felt isolated in her stare. "I trusted you because you're new, so I assumed you're not caught up in any of this yet." Before Harold could reply, Manu interrupted once again.

"He's actually more caught up than you think," he said proudly, "he's found another community of people and a factory and all sorts. Tell her, Harold." Franziska punched Harold on the arm, making him flinch.

Harold proceeded to tell Sarah about everything he'd found a few nights ago, as well as being invited to Christian's complex before that. As she took some time to process what he told her, Sarah closed her eyes in concentration. Seeing an opportunity, Harold looked her up and down. She must have been in her early twenties but looked extremely athletic. Her tank top and leggings revealed her slender figure, which Harold struggled not to enjoy. Feeling an immediate and horrendous sense of shame, he covered his eyes, pretending to be lost in thought.

"Can you take me there? To the factory, and to this other community?"

"Um, sure," said Harold nervously, "if we go tomorrow night, we can plan ahead an-"

"Tonight," Sarah said sternly, "right now. But we can't all go, it'll be too suspicious." At this, Manu raised his hand, telling the group he was happy to stay behind and cover for them, to which Franziska agreed.

The group devised a plan: they'd put the record on in Harold's room to make it seem as though he was in, and if anybody asked where Sarah was, Manu would explain that he'd seen her knocking at Harold's door. With the four in agreement, they put their plan into action, and Harold lead Sarah into the darkness of the square and up towards the woods.

Along the way, Sarah didn't say much. Whenever Harold tried to strike up a conversation, she replied by either giving him a one-word answer, or murmuring a sound of agreement. After a while of traipsing through the woodland, which was still wet underfoot, the two made it to the factory. Sat in darkness, there was nobody inside, and the sound Harold had heard the last time he was here was absent. Harold explained how it had been in operation a few days ago, and how he'd seen several people in blue aprons by the doorway. Crouched low to the floor in case anybody was around, the two investigated the outside of the factory, but other than a branch wedged into the floor by one of the windows, they found nothing. Sarah tried the window that the branch lead up to, but it was locked from the inside, so she instructed Harold to guide her to the community he'd found. Sarah seemed full of confidence, without an ounce of fear in the way she spoke or acted. Although he'd met her only a few hours before, Harold already felt himself developing a soft spot for Sarah – something that clearly wasn't reciprocated. He wondered how Maria would react if she found out he had feelings for someone else, which made him feel guilty. Although he knew she'd had relations with someone else, he didn't think he had it in him to pursue anything with Sarah - not that she'd given him any indication of a mutual feeling.

The chill of the night had started to creep in, but before long the two were on the path that lead directly into the second town. Feeling brave with his new hat, he gestured for Sarah to stay behind him, which she reluctantly agreed to. Careful not to make any loud noises or draw attention to themselves, the two crept their way towards the opening. As they got closer, Harold stopped, listening out for any sounds from the space ahead, but to his surprise he heard nothing. Not only this, but he couldn't see any light at all as the community he'd seen came into view. The buildings were there, as well as the shed that Harold had spent the night in, but there was nobody around. Confused as to what was happening, Harold stood up, ignoring Sarah's plea to stay low and quiet.

He wandered into the town, looking around for any sign of life. The buildings were all the same as he'd seen them previously, but they looked deserted. Soon, Sarah joined his search, all but abandoning their stealthy approach. She noticed that the door to one of the buildings was open, so she went to take a look inside. Meanwhile, Harold stood in the centre of the community, where all he could hear was the sound of the wind rustling through the trees. There was nobody there; not the woman he'd spoken to, nor anybody else. He slowly turned his head, hoping to find something that would prove what he'd seen, but there was nothing.

Soon, Sarah made her way out of the building and over to Harold.

"Harold, this is a dead end, look."

A vacant expression came over his face. Harold couldn't believe what he was seeing. She was holding up her finger, revealing a thick layer of dust on it. Nobody had been here for some time, both Sarah and Harold knew it.

Chapter 9:
Questions.

"Manu, do you ever wonder if you've made the right decisions in life?"

"Of course," replied the Italian, his hands behind his head, a cigarette hanging loosely from his lips, "but I used to love the Tasmanian Devil, so I thought a tattoo would be appropriate."

"Not about your rubbish tattoo, Manu, about everything. I mean, what got you here, what you've done in life, all of that."

"Hmm, not really. Because, you know, I can't change it now. And if I wish I could, the only person it'd upset is me. So, I think it's best to just accept it and move on. You can't change the past, but you can change the future."

Franziska cuddled up to Manu, who still laid with his hands behind his head. He knew that she was worried about Harold and Sarah on their trip to the factory, but he figured there was no point getting her worked up about it.

After a short while, he could feel Franziska twitching in her sleep, still holding him around his stomach. Ever since the two had started their relationship, Manu had noticed how Franziska didn't sleep well, often twitching and jolting in her sleep. He wondered what kind of dreams she had, and how they made her move in such strange ways. In an attempt to ease her twitching, he began to play with her hair. As the strands of hair slid between his fingers, he lightly massaged her head – something that usually helped her fall into a deeper sleep. Within moments, the twitching stopped, and the snoring began.

By the time morning came, Franziska was still clutching Manu's stomach, dribbling on his t-shirt. As he carefully slipped away and climbed over her, he wrote her a note explaining where he was going. He changed his clothes, kissed her on the cheek, and made his way to the square outside.

The weather had once again taken a turn for the worse, and although it hadn't started raining yet, it looked as if it soon would. The grey sky above gave way to thick black clouds in the distance, and the wind kicked all sorts of gravel and sticks up into the air. Apart from the sounds of the sea crashing against the rocks nearby, there was nothing. No seagulls, no people, nothing. It was eerily quiet, which unsettled Manu. Pulling his jacket tight around him, he made his way down the steps to the docks to watch the waves.

For the first time in a while, Manu had his hair down, flowing behind him as he approached the docks. It reminded him of the day he arrived on the island, full of self-doubt and terrified beyond belief. He felt as though he came to the island as a boy, but had since become a man, and although he missed the food and music of his home country, he felt comfortable.

As he sat down on the docks facing the sea, he crossed his legs and closed his eyes, letting the spray of the water hit his face. He thought about Harold and Sarah, wondering if they'd found the people Harold had seen, and what would happen if they had. He wondered if it would change the way he lived, and how Franziska would react if things began to change again for her. Soon after, he began to wonder what he'd do if they didn't return. In many ways, Harold had been right – people disappearing from the island was bad, and it should concern him. Yet all Manu had wanted was someone like Franziska and a simple life - something he had right now. He thought about the way Harold had spoken of his life before, when they'd been sorting the new hats, and he imagined what it would be like if he and Franziska had a life like that. A normal job, friends, family, and a real place to call home.

Hearing footsteps from behind him, Manu half-expected to see Franziska joining him, but was surprised to see that Christian, dressed as smartly as ever, was making his way towards him. He rose to his feet and offered a smile, which Christian returned. Christian held out his hand and greeted Manu, before gesturing for Manu to sit back down. Christian joined him, struggling to cross his legs in his suit trousers, before resorting to sitting with his legs stretched out in front of him.

"Manu, I'm worried about Harold," said Christian, his voice sounding sincere and genuinely troubled.

"Harold? Why?" Manu hoped that Christian didn't know of their sleuthing the night before and tried his best to sound innocent.

"He hasn't seemed himself for the past few days. He's been distant, keeping to himself. I hope he's alright." Trying his best to put Christian's suspicions to bed, Manu thought of the most convincing lie he could.

"We shared a drink last night, he seemed fine. Maybe he's just missing home?"

"Aren't we all?" Came the reply. Christian extended his arms backwards, leaning onto them and looking up at the sky.

The two sat quietly for a while, listening to the steadily increasing sounds of the waves, slapping against the rocks around them. Manu wondered why Christian had joined him, and thought maybe he was just looking for company, but didn't want to ask. Then, out of nowhere, Christian spoke again.

"I feel as though the community here is beginning to fracture. I don't know what it is, but I can feel it in my bones," Christian turned his head towards Manu, "I'm thinking of throwing a party of some type at my place tonight, you know? Invite all the residents, give people a chance to let their hair down. What do you think?" Unsure of how to respond, Manu began to speak without thinking.

"Yeah, sure, that sounds great."

"Would you care to ask Harold and Franzi? Seeing as you're close to them both. I feel as though they're more likely to say yes to you, than if I ask."

Manu was taken aback by the way Christian was talking to him. He usually came across as very sure of himself, speaking with confidence and authority. Yet, right now, he seemed unsure and timid, almost as if something had changed within him.

"Of course," said Manu, "When I see them, I'll ask."

Later that day, as Manu took both his and Franziska's laundry to the basement of his building, he heard someone shuffle into the washing room soon after him. Peeking over his shoulder he could see it was Sarah. Manu wondered why she was here, as she had a washing room in the red brick building, but kept to himself until she approached the washing machine beside him.

"Have you seen Harold?" she asked, careful to keep her voice low.

"What do you mean? He was with you."

"He was, but I lost him."

"Lost him?" Manu said furiously, trying his best to keep his voice at a whisper, "how could you lose him?"

"There was nobody there, Manu, nobody. It was a fucking ghost town."

"And the factory?"

"There was nobody there either. When we didn't find anybody at the town, I told him we should try the factory, but he insisted on staying. By the time I returned, I couldn't find him. But I'm telling you, Manu, thick dust, rust everywhere, there's no way anybody's been there for years."

"But Harold spoke to somebody?"

At that moment, Mrs. Sands came into the room holding an empty basket. Both Manu and Sarah stayed silent, loading their clothes into the machines as Mrs. Sands placed her basket onto the pile in the corner, and left.

"So he says," replied Sarah. Manu dropped his basket to the floor and turned towards the exit.

"I'm going to find him," said Manu, "do me a favour and finish up mine, will you?" He pointed at the basket of dirty clothes he'd left, "and careful with the delicates." As he was about to make his way up the stairs, he remembered Christian's party. He popped his head back into the washing room, checking that Sarah was still alone, and gave her the details, telling her to speak to him if she found Harold before he did.

Manu made his way into the square, the dark clouds now hanging overhead, threatening to bring along a thunderous storm. He strolled into the red brick building and up to Harold's room, knocking firmly at the door. After hearing no response, he tried the doorknob, but it didn't budge. Seeing no other option, Manu checked to his left and right to make sure nobody was around, pulled out two hairpins out of his back pocket, and placed them into the lock. After some twisting and turning, it clicked open. Pushing open the door in a hurry, Manu saw Harold frantically writing on the walls of his room.

He looked deranged, having clearly not washed from the night before, his eyes darting about the room with his hands following them. His hair was greasy and the dirt under his fingernails was a thick black shade. Looking up at the walls, Manu could see that Harold had been writing the names Jerry and Yvette over and over again, as well as drawing the factory, some kind of town, and a bald-headed figure, along with various other scribblings. He hadn't noticed Manu in the doorway and continued to dash about the small space, adding words, crossing out sections, and drawing small pictures.

Manu closed the door behind him slowly, hoping that his friend would take notice of him, but he didn't. His eyes kept dashing from one side to the other, as if he were possessed.

"Harold? Harold, it's Manu. What are you doing?"

Harold didn't respond. He continued to exist in his own little bubble, concentrating on everything and nothing at the same time. Seeing no other option, Manu tentatively made his way over to Harold, ready for him to snap at any moment, but he didn't. Manu was now within touching distance of his friend, but he still didn't react. Extending his arm to grab Harold's hand, he still expected his friend to lash out at him. Manu slowly pulled Harold's hand away from the wall. Seeing that Harold already seemed calmer, Manu tried again.

"Little man, are you OK?"

"No," said Harold, his voice warbling and trembling, "No I'm not."

"What happened?" asked Manu, not expecting a comprehensive answer.

"It's Christian," Harold said, turning his head slowly towards Manu, "I think he's making us eat people. I think we've eaten Jerry and Yvette."

Chapter 10:
Party.

After Harold had showered and made himself presentable, Manu sat him down and asked him to describe what he'd seen the night before. He explained that after Sarah had gone to explore the factory, he'd found body bags and butchers equipment in one of the buildings of the town, as well as several large wheelbarrows.

"Christian told me that Mrs. Sands' chicken burgers are actually pork, but what if they're not?" he asked. "What if they're the missing residents? You told me that she doesn't set up all the time, maybe that's why?"

"Harold," said Manu, frowning, "It's a bit of a stretch, don't you think? Why would he do that?"

"Look around you!" shouted Harold as his arms flung into the air. "We're on a fucking island in the middle of nowhere filled with criminals! Do you really think having a cannibal leader is the craziest idea?"

Manu looked at the scribblings on the walls around him, trying to make sense of what his friend had written.

"Let's say you're right, Harold, then what? What do we do next?"

"We expose him for the monster he is!"

"Harold, I'm not sure that's the best idea. We don't have any solid proof."

Harold stood up and followed the lines he'd drawn onto the walls, linking random words and pictures to each other. He connected the words 'complex' and 'Jerry', before turning back towards Manu with a grin on his face.

"I think he's storing the bodies in his complex. I've seen it, lots of buildings surrounding the lighthouse. Either the bodies are in there, or the people I saw at the town are."

"I'm not saying I believe you," said Manu reluctantly, "but he's invited all the residents there for a party tonight. Maybe we cou-"

"Excellent!" Interrupted Harold, "We'll get into them tonight in front of everybody and expose that freak!"

Harold came up with the basics of a plan and ran through it with Manu several times. When they'd agreed on a time to meet, Manu asked that Harold sleep on his theory before committing, to which he agreed. They said their goodbyes, and Manu left, leaving Harold to rest within the graffitied walls of his room. Although he rested, Harold couldn't sleep. His head was spinning with possibilities, linking his theory with what he'd seen and heard. He knew he was right and would do anything to prove it.

So as not to arouse suspicion, he combed his hair back and wore his nicest clothes. He figured that the better he fit in, the easier it'd be to sleuth around at the party. He hadn't fully figured out his plan yet, but he had an idea, and would act on instinct when the time arose.

He met up with Manu, Franziska, and Sarah by the fountain later that night, and after brief greetings, the group made their way up the path towards the complex. Harold was surprised that none of the group asked where he'd been since yesterday, but figured that Manu had filled them in on the details. As they made their way towards the lighthouse, they saw a few of the other residents ahead of them between the large trees that littered the sides of the path. It had already started to get dark, but somebody had placed lamps along some of the trees, illuminating the way. As the lighthouse came into view, Harold was surprised at just how many people were already mingling outside. The only person he recognised was Charlie, due to his large stature and round afro towering above everybody else.

A large fire burned in the middle of the complex, the dancing flames flickering light in all directions, creating large shadows on the buildings around them. At one side Harold could see Mrs. Sands' stall, handing out rolls to the residents, which made the hair on his arms stand to attention. He wanted to tell people what they were really eating, but he didn't want to jump the gun. He felt his heart begin to beat harder and faster as the rage built inside of him, but with his fists and jaw clenched, he kept his composure. He looked over to Manu, who directed a timid smile back at him, showing Harold that he'd noticed it too.

For the next few hours, the group mingled with the residents. Somebody had attached a large speaker to a record player, which bellowed out some kind of pop music Harold didn't recognise. Inside the bar-like building Harold had been in before, he noticed the two sisters talking to Christian. Harold was in two minds as to whether he should make the effort to talk to them or not. If he did, it'd make it seem as though he was comfortable, lowering Christian's guard, but in that case, there was no guarantee he'd be able to contain his emotions.

Before he could decide, Christian called him over, making the decision for him. As Harold made his way over, he could see that

Christian once again had his sleeves rolled up, revealing his scarred arms. He smiled as though he was genuinely happy to see Harold, but Harold knew he saw right through the facade.

"Harold, my friend! You remember the girls, Gill and Daisy. We've missed you! Where have you been? I feel as though I've barely seen you the last few days. Are you OK?"

Trying his best not to let his true emotions show, Harold took a deep breath before answering.

"Hey, girls. Sorry, Christian. I've just been keeping to myself lately. Everything has been a bit," he paused for a moment to think, "overwhelming. I'm sure you can appreciate that."

"Oh, absolutely," said Christian, seemingly genuinely relieved, "I'm just glad you're alright, and I'm glad you made it. Can I get you something to drink, maybe a bite to eat?"

"No!" cried Harold, causing several of the residents to turn their heads towards him. "Sorry," he said, more calmly, "no, thank you. I've had a bit of a funny belly lately. I'm just going to stick to water if that's alright."

Looking a mixture of confused and scared, Christian nodded. "Of course," he said, his arm now placed on Harold's shoulder. "Girls, do you mind? I want to speak to Harold alone." The girls made their way towards the bar, leaving Harold and Christian alone in the corner of the room.

Christian swirled his drink in his hand before taking a sip. Harold noticed that he looked stressed, and not as comfortable and confident as he usually did. He wondered if he somehow knew about his plan, but hoped for the best.

"Harold, I know things can be tough, but you know you've always got me, right?"

"What do you mean?" asked Harold calmly.

"I know that this place can be a bit – overwhelming. It can be lonely, confusing, scary, and everything in-between. But that's why it's important that we stick together. That's why we should always have each other's back, helping each other to get back up when we fall down."

Harold knew Christian was getting at something but wasn't sure exactly what. He stayed quiet, allowing Christian to continue.

"I need you to do me a favour," he said, "I need you to find Charlie and tell him he has to open the shop a little early tomorrow. He won't be happy, but you can tell him that the captain is bringing him some goodies nice and early, so he'll need to be open."

Harold reluctantly agreed, acting the part of Christian's friend. He knew that, after consoling him during his episode a few days ago, Christian would be less suspicious if he thought Harold was his friend. So, he trudged over to the door and looked around for Charlie. He wasn't hard to find, as he stood head and shoulders taller than more or less everybody at the party. As Harold made his way over to the man he barely knew, he saw Manu, Franziska, and Sarah sat together, drinking and laughing. If he didn't know any better, Harold would have thought they were genuinely having fun. Whilst he was full of rage and anger, the people he considered his best chance of revealing the truth were having fun and playing about.

Approaching Charlie, Harold cleared his throat in an over-the-top manner, grabbing the large man's attention. As confidently as he could, Harold delivered the message from Christian. Looking visibly annoyed, Charlie sighed and accepted the request. As Harold was ready to re-group with his friends, a thought popped into his head – he hadn't ever seen Charlie tending to a shop or stall of any kind.

"Charlie, which shop do you run? I've been here for a bit now, but I've never seen your shop."

"Really? Normally people joke about how they can't *not* see me towering over the desk," he laughed, "it's the little brown building at the end of the path, off of the market.

"You mean just like Jerry's shop?"

"Jerry's shop?" asked the giant. "Jerry never had a shop?"

Harold couldn't understand what Charlie was saying. He knew Jerry had owned a shop, as he'd been in there on his first full day on the island. What he'd seen in there had started the whole mess Harold found himself in now. Desperate to sort out what he assumed was confusion, Harold began to describe what he'd seen in his friends shop.

"Lobster cages. Hanging from the ceiling. No decorations on the outside like the houses around it." Harold spoke erratically, taking sharp breaths between most words.

"So, you *have* been in my shop? When was this? I'd have given you a neighbour discount," chuckled Charlie.

Harold couldn't understand what he was hearing. As he began to stumble away from Charlie towards his friends, his vision started to blur. Instead of the people around him, drinking and having fun, all he could see was Jerry in his shop, just as he'd seen him on his first full day on the island.

The moment he'd gone into the storeroom kept playing out in front of him, over and over. He could hear the sound of Jerry's voice, first as clear as day, slowly becoming more and more echoed, as if he was travelling through a large tunnel. The image of Jerry behind the counter became distorted and warped, like it was melting before his very eyes. Stretched out of proportion and bent into another dimension, as if the image was curving and wrapping around itself. Jerry's voice suddenly became extremely deep and demonic, thundering through to Harold's core and shaking his bones.

Harold couldn't concentrate on any one thing he could see. Whilst the image of his friend was now almost completely unrecognisable, he couldn't focus on any specific part, almost as if his eyes wouldn't allow him the luxury of comprehending what was happening. He felt something hard crash against his knees, but as he looked down all he could see was the distorted vision of the wooden flooring of Jerry's shop. What was once a dark brown and chipped wooden floor was now a purple, blurry patch of what looked like rubber beneath his feet.

As he tried to focus on his friend's voice, another sound began to fill the vision. It started as a low-level hum, but quickly grew to what sounded like somebody trying to call Harold's name. Harold wanted to respond, but as he tried to open his mouth, his lips refused to move. They felt as if they'd been sewn together, not parting even the slightest bit. The harder he tried, the tighter they felt. All he could manage was a kind of guttural yell, exhaling heavily through his noise as he tried desperately to open his mouth.

What had once been an image of his friend behind the counter of his shop was now completely unrecognisable. All Harold could see was a mixture of shapes and colours, that felt both meaningless and intimidating to Harold. Jerry's voice was now just a low buzz of a noise that felt as though it was cutting through to Harold's soul, tormenting and torturing him. He tried once again to make some kind of noise, but his lips still wouldn't move.

Suddenly, Harold felt a splash of something cold hit him square in the face. His eyes quickly rolled into the back of his head, before snapping back to their normal position. The vision had gone, and instead he could see that he was kneeling on the path outside with the residents staring at him. Manu was crouched next to him, an empty glass pointed in Harold's direction. Before he could say anything, Manu picked him up by the arm and lead them down the path towards the square, the residents remaining silent with their eyes fixed on the pair.

When they were out of sight, Manu stood Harold bolt upright, looking him straight in the eyes. He explained to Harold that he'd seen him go into some kind of frenzy, making strange noises and shaking his head. He told him how he'd seen him collapse to his knees in front of everybody, and that's when the Italian had interviewed by throwing his drink over him.

"It was Charlie," said Harold, trying to get his bearings together, "he said that Jerry didn't own the shop. But I was there, Manu, you know I was. The old brown one with the lobster cages. You know he owned that shop!"

Manu's eyes dropped downward, as if he was ashamed or scared.

"No, he didn't, Harold. Jerry has never run a shop here."

"Yes, he did!" Insisted Harold, pushing Manu away. "I was in there and I saw him disappear! I told you this and you believed me!" By now, Harold had broken into a sweat, exhaling deeply through his nose.

"You told me he disappeared into a stockroom, but I assumed you were lost in the moment and got your words mixed up. He's never run a shop here, Harold. I'm telling you."

Harold couldn't understand what was going on. Doubts flooded his mind as he tried to scramble together a logical explanation. He knew that he was right, no matter what people were telling him. He knew that somehow, Christian was behind everything that was happening, and that the answers were in the buildings surrounding the lighthouse. Before he could think any more about it, he broke into a sprint and made his way towards the complex. Manu called out to him, but Harold ignored his pleas. Before long Harold could hear footsteps not far behind him, and a brief look over his shoulder revealed that Manu was sprinting after him.

As Harold approached the complex once again, he saw that people were still dancing and enjoying themselves, unaware of what was contained in the buildings around them. He had wanted to wait until everybody was inside so he could check before the big reveal, but he no longer had that luxury. With the earlier episode and Manu now hot on his heels, he knew it was now or never.

Harold weaved between the residents as he decided which of the buildings to open, finally choosing the largest one with several wires and cables leading to it. As he made his way to the wooden door of the building, he tried to open it, realising there was a large padlock keeping the door shut. He tried to pull it open, but was tackled to the floor by Manu, his head slamming onto the stone below. For a second or so, Harold couldn't focus on what had happened, but he soon regained his consciousness. He kicked Manu off of him and threw a fist in his direction, making contact with the Italian's nose and breaking it instantly. As Manu cradled his face, he cried out in agony, and almost every resident at the party was now facing Harold. Unfazed by the attention, Harold called out for Christian, his voice sounding like he was challenging his mortal enemy to a fight to the death.

Before long, Christian emerged from the crowd, his hands raised in surrender. Though his posture suggested he was ready to give up, his face said otherwise.

"Harold, whatever it is you're doing, now is the time to stop. Apologise to Manu, apologise to everybody here, and go home."

Christian's intonation only angered Harold more, and his voice became raspier and more menacing.

"I'm going to expose you for who you really are, Christian. You're a liar, you're a murderer, and more importantly, you're a fucking cannibal!"

The crowd let out a collective gasp, whispering amongst themselves at Harold's statement.

"Harold, my friend, the island has gotten to you," said Christian calmly as he stepped towards Harold, "you've had a few traumatic days, and now you've hit your head. Please, I beg of you, calm yourself down, and let's talk about this."

"The talking is done, Christian. You killed my friend, and then you did something to him in that factory you've got hidden away, and now you're making us eat him! That's how Mrs. Sands gets the meat!"

Some of the residents screamed at Harold's news, whilst others shook their heads.

"Listen to me Harold, you're sick. You were sick before you even arrived here. Now, if you want help, we can help you. But you have to stop being erratic and calm down."

"I'm going to expose you!" screamed Harold. Manu was still laying on the floor cradling his face, and as Franziska made her way over to help him, she made Harold jump. Christian took advantage of Harold's lapse in concentration to move closer to him, which Harold quickly noticed.

"Very well, Harold, you've left me no choice."

From Harold's feet, Manu looked over to Christian. He shook his head, asking him not to do what he was preparing, but it was already too late. Christian stood on a nearby bench and addressed the crowd, his arms outstretched like a preacher.

"Our good friend Harold has decided to take matters into his own hands. As Franziska found out not too long ago, this is not how we do things here." Even Harold was fixated on Christian by now, and with one hand firmly on the padlocked door, he stood listening to the charismatic leader of the island. "But you see, he is not the kind, timid man you think he is. Although his actions here tonight may have cast some doubt on your opinion of Harold, perhaps his past will help to clear things up." Harold began to shake with anger, but decided he'd do better holding his position rather than attacking Christian. He had no choice but to let the man finish his speech. "Growing jealous of his wife's affair, Harold attacked his wife's lover, brutally beating him and leaving him for dead." His voice bellowed out towards the crowd, who stood silent, listening to his every word. "He was not only a poor husband, but a jealous and violent one. So, please, do not judge him for his actions here tonight. As, although it may seem out of character, it is not. Our friend, Harold Kobbs, is clearly an unstable and paranoid person. And he is beyond our help."

Scared that the crowd would soon turn on him, Harold picked up a nearby stone and began bashing at the lock of the door. The residents closest to him all jumped out of their skin, but within a few hits the lock broke loose.

"Paranoid or not, at least I'm right!" shouted Harold ecstatically, as if he'd drawn a lethal blow to his opponent. He pulled open the door to reveal the darkness inside, and he knew that, despite not being able to see what was inside the building, he had the audience's attention. "Christian, why don't you go in there and show us what we've all been eating?" he said confidently. Christian jumped down from the bench and made his way inside, not reaching for the light switch beside him. He briefly disappeared into the darkness, and Harold heard him struggle to pick up something heavy. He faced out towards the crowd of people surrounding them, smiling proudly as he knew what was about to happen.

"Here you go, Harold, you win," said Christian from inside the darkness. As he emerged into the light, Harold's eyes widened – Christian was carrying an entire dead pig. Christian smiled confidently, the same way Harold had done moments ago. "You win, my friend, you've exposed me. The chicken rolls are actually pork schnitzel rolls." The crowd watched silently as Christian hauled the dead pig onto the stone outside and dropped it to the floor. He turned towards Harold, who was still watching with his mouth open, and smiled once again. "Life is like a game of chess, Harold," he said sarcastically.

Without thinking, Harold turned and ran back down the path towards the square, only this time he didn't look behind him. It didn't sound like anybody following him, but he couldn't hear much over the noise of his shoes clashing against the stone and his heart beating faster than he'd ever felt before. He could feel his heartbeat in every inch of his being, stretching right up to his ears.

He couldn't understand what was happening or how he'd got it wrong. Just a few hours ago he was convinced he had it all figured out, and now he wasn't sure if anything he'd seen or heard was true. As he sprinted past the square and down the path past the shop, he didn't know where exactly he was heading. The only place he figured he could go was the abandoned town he'd been to before, although now he was doubting that he'd even seen it at all. Not slowing to avoid the sticks and branches below his feet, he stumbled as the path gave way to the grass of the forest. Adrenaline coursed through his veins as he skipped and jumped over logs and muddy patches, his focus set on getting as far away from the people of the island as possible. He no longer had a plan or strategy for what to do next – all he had was himself, and now he was beginning to doubt even that.

He passed the factory and began down the path to the second town, half expecting that to have been something he imagined too. But as he saw the moonlight reflecting off the glass panes of the hanging lanterns, he knew he'd reached the town. He could see that it was still abandoned and figured he must have imagined the people he'd seen and the woman he'd spoken to – no matter how real it had all seemed. With no plan of any kind to follow, he darted into the shed he'd slept in before and huddled up under the sheets inside.

Now he was alone, he had time to think, but the more he thought, the more he doubted himself. He couldn't understand what had gone wrong or why this was happening. He knew he'd seen Jerry in his shop, and he knew that the building would reveal the bodies, or remains, of the missing residents. Instead, he'd become the island's lunatic, leaving behind the few people he trusted, and now had nothing. He wasn't sure what he'd do next, but he knew he had to rest. Feeling somewhat safe in the privacy of the shed, he closed his eyes and tried to settle down.

After just a few minutes, Harold heard footsteps outside. It sounded like just one person, but he couldn't be sure. He stayed still, hoping that the footsteps would soon walk away and leave him be, but instead they came closer. As they approached the door to the shed, Harold laid dead still. The door opened, and in stepped the stranger.

"Harold, I know you're here."

Chapter 11:
Sarah.

Sarah could see Manu carry Harold down the path back towards the square. She wasn't sure if what she'd seen had been part of Harold's plan, but it had all happened so quickly that she hadn't had a chance to slip away. She was worried that she'd blown it, and that she'd now have to improvise.

Christian addressed the crowd briefly, reminding them all that they were there to enjoy themselves. More than happy to hear this, everyone went back to partying almost immediately. They were laughing, singing, dancing, and drinking. Sarah tailed Christian for a short while as he made his way back indoors, but when she saw that he simply continued to mingle with the sisters, she gave up. Pouring herself another drink to blend in, she looked around for Manu's return, but he was nowhere to be found. She wasn't sure about the Italian and his involvement in their plan to expose what was happening to the residents. Whenever he spoke, Sarah couldn't help but feel he wasn't committed, and that somehow, he was just along for the ride.

As she stepped back outside, the intimidating stature of Charlie stuck out like a sore thumb. Hoping to get some answers as to what had caused Harold's meltdown, Sarah approached him and asked what had been said. He explained how Harold had insisted that his shop belonged to Jerry, and then began to stumble off, before suffering the episode that the crowd had seen. Sarah thanked Charlie for his time, and began to snoop around in plain sight, hidden by the crowd enjoying themselves.

She approached the door of a small building on the outside of the complex. The wooden door was padlocked like the rest and sat next to the largest of the outside buildings, which had various electric cables connected to it. She wasn't sure why, but something attracted her to this specific building. While nobody was looking, she began to try and pry open the padlock, but before she got close, she heard the sound of somebody running as the crowd grew silent. Looking over her shoulder, she could see that it was Harold, sprinting back to the party, with Manu not far behind him. Seeing her opportunity, Sarah slipped away between the buildings and into the woods out of sight. She wasn't sure what exactly Harold was up to or why Manu was chasing him, but she trusted he knew what he was doing. She made her way through the woods until she found the path to the square and made her way back to the town as quickly as she could.

When she arrived at the square, it was completely vacant. The distant sound of music had stopped, so whatever Harold had done at the party must have worked Besides the waves crashing against the rocks and the wind whistling between the buildings, Sarah could hear nothing. She made her way up to Harold's room and used the key he'd given her the night they'd gone looking for the second town. As instructed, she searched through the desk until she found the letter he'd written. Hoping to read it, Sarah was disappointed to see that it'd already been sealed, and there was no way of opening it without Maria knowing it'd been read. Suppressing her curiosity, she slid it into her jacket pocket alongside her own letter, locked the room, and made her way back outside to continue her mission.

As she carefully stepped outside, Sarah stopped in her tracks. She heard what sounded like footsteps coming from the path towards

Christian's complex. They hadn't quite reached the square yet, but there was no way she'd make it to the path down to the docks unnoticed. She dived towards the fountain, ducking down next to the stone structure for cover. As the footsteps got closer, she peered around the curved structure, hoping to see whoever it was before they saw her. To Sarah's surprise, it was two men she hadn't seen before, one significantly taller than the other. Looking closer, she could tell that they were intoxicated, their legs barely managing to keep them upright. As they made their way past the fountain and towards the red brick building, they were completely oblivious to Sarah. She wasn't particularly well-hidden, but the two were so drunk that they strolled right past her without batting an eyelid. They spoke as if they were pretending to be on a TV show, occasionally imitating a Geordie accent and repeatedly saying the name Mikey. Sarah wondered if this was Ben and Peter, two people Harold said he'd met on his first day on the island, but as the two entered the red brick building, they closed the door behind them and were out of sight. Sarah waited a moment to ensure nobody else had left the party early before making her way down the path between the buildings and towards the dock.

Ahead of her to one side of the docks was a large trunk, full of items for the captain to take to the mainland. Sarah hoped that the captain had been telling the truth about taking things back without consulting Christian. She placed Harold's letter inside, tucking it under a small parcel so that it was somewhat hidden. She then took out her own letter, addressed to Donald, and kissed it before hiding it in a similar way. As she thought about how it might be the last time she'd get to communicate with him, a single tear rolled down her cheek and onto the roof of the trunk as she closed it.

The wind kicked up again, blowing her hair in front of her face as she made her way back to the square. By the time she emerged from between the two buildings, people had gathered in small groups around the fountain, all of them looking concerned and scared. Among them she could see Franziska holding an unstable Manu, who was doubled over with a hand pressed to his face. As Sarah got closer, she could see drops of claret trickling down Manu's fingers as he clasped them around his nose. Sarah comforted them, asking what had happened, to which Manu simply removed his hand. Whilst the top of his nose bridge sat where it should, it curved off sharply to one side, and his nostrils were coated with blood. With his hand away from his face, the blood began to slide down through his moustache and onto his lips. Noticing the disgusted look on Sarah's face, he smiled, as if to tell her he was fine.

"What happened?" asked Sarah, feeling as though she knew the answer already. Before Manu could reply, Franziska spoke, an air of anger in her voice.

"Harold happened. He's gone fucking psycho and run off. I knew we shouldn't have gotten involved, Manu. I fucking told you." Sarah began to speak, but Franziska whisked Manu away and lead him into their building before she got a chance to say anything. Looking around her, she could see that the residents were clearly shaken by whatever had happened at the complex, but not to the degree that Sarah and Harold had hoped. She assumed the worst, fearing that Harold hadn't managed to expose Christian. She began to doubt what Harold believed, but she tried to stay positive. If Harold had survived the encounter, she knew where he'd be.

Sarah changed, grabbed a bite to eat, and left to find Harold. As she began down the path towards the woods, a voice called out to her from behind. It was Christian, who stood proud as punch, looking at her accusingly.

"I didn't see too much of you at the party, is everything OK?" he asked sincerely, the suspicious look still in his eyes. She frantically thought of a plausible excuse before responding.

"I'm fine," she said coolly, "I saw that Ben and Peter had maybe had a bit too much to drink, so I wanted to make sure they got home safely. Why, did I miss much?" Sarah was convinced that her lie had worked as Christian's expression changed from one of accusation to one of playfulness.

"You could say that you missed something truly memorable, but don't worry. I'm sure there'll be another occasion." He slowly stepped towards her. The closer he got, the more Sarah could see the sweat that was dripping down from his hairline to his ears. "How are you though, Sarah? Are you settling in well?"

"Fine," she responded as quickly as she could, trying to get away from the conversation. "I'm all good. Everything is just a bit overwhelming, you know? Thought I'd go for a walk, clear my head and stuff."

"I used to know someone like you, Sarah," he laughed, "I liked her a lot." Christian began to look at Sarah longingly, but before he could continue, she turned away and carried on down the path, occasionally checking over her shoulder to ensure she wasn't followed.

A short way into the woods, she heard the snapping of twigs underfoot from nearby. Checking that it wasn't of her own doing, she stopped, and sure enough, the sounds continued. Fearful that Christian had followed her, she ducked behind a nearby tree and scanned the area for the source of the sound. She soon spotted a few of the residents, Doctor Halter, Felix, and a few others she didn't know the names of, were trampling through the forest a short distance away from her. They were making their way towards the factory building. As Sarah began to hope that Harold wasn't there, she noticed that the group was putting on blue aprons and face masks, making them almost completely unrecognisable. She wondered if these were who Harold had seen in the small town away from the factory, but before long, the group had disappeared through the trees.

It was getting dark, and Sarah knew she'd have to find Harold soon, or risk him disappearing, along with her father and the other unfortunate victims. Harold's plan had thus far failed, and she wasn't sure how finding him would help the situation, but she knew she'd feel a lot more comfortable if she did, so she continued through the woods towards where she thought he'd be – the second town.

It was now getting dark, and Sarah struggled to see particularly far in front of her. Careful not to make as much noise as the others had, she timidly stepped over branches and through muddy patches, trying her best to remain silent. She'd decided to take a different route in order to avoid encountering the group again and steered well clear of the factory to reduce her risk of being caught. However, as she began to step around a large fallen tree, she felt something hard crunch beneath her foot. She raised her shoulders and scrunched up her eyes, hoping and praying that nobody else had heard the sound. Pausing for a few seconds, holding herself as still as she could, she assumed that no one had heard, and finally began to relax. She lifted her foot to investigate the source of the noise, but was surprised to see what looked like something vaguely shiny buried in the mud beneath her. She dug around the sides of the object to loosen it, and as she pulled it out of the mud, she knew immediately what it was – an expelled bullet casing. She rolled it around in her hand for a while, trying to see what type it was, but it was too weathered and warped to see exactly what it was. She began to search the ground around her for more and found three more casings. She wasn't sure exactly what had happened, but she knew it wasn't good. She began to wonder if she'd bitten off more than she could chew by coming to the island, and she now considered abandoning her mission entirely. She pushed the collection of casings into her pocket and continued with the only plan she had – to find Harold.

Chapter 12:
Christian.

As Christian examined himself in the mirror, he could see that a few fine hairs sat just above his lip like the fuzz on a peach. Happy with the first signs of manhood, he ran downstairs to find his father, but he was nowhere to be seen. He called out to him but heard no response, and wondered if he'd gone out early to attend to his chores.

Christian stepped outside, and the brisk morning air hit him like a ton of bricks. He'd been hoping for a white winter, but any chance of snow soon turned to rain, and as it fast approached Christmas, Christian began to wonder if he'd see any snow this side of the holiday. The people outside went about their routines; taking their dirty clothes to be cleaned, talking to their friends, or just enjoying the morning. When he and his father first moved here, Christian had mostly kept to himself, but he was growing more comfortable with his new home. As he strolled past everybody, he greeted them with a large grin, to which most of the residents responded with a smile of their own. Christian almost completely missed Mrs. Sands, so she ruffled his hair as he went by, making him jump. The two chatted briefly as they did most mornings, asking each other how they'd slept and what dreams they'd had. Mrs. Sands, who must've bee in her late 40's, had become both a mother figure and a best friend of sorts to Christian. The two often spent evenings together chatting about everything and nothing.

"Look at this," Christian said enthusiastically, pointing at the wispy hairs above his lip, "my moustache has started to grow!"

"Wow!" replied Mrs. Sands sarcastically, unbeknownst to Christian. "Would you look at that! Soon your moustache will be bigger than Mr. Sands'!"

Christian laughed excitedly, happy that he could finally show off some kind of facial hair to somebody. "I don't want one like his, it's too big and bushy! But look, it's growing all the way along!" Once again, he pointed towards his lip. "So, hopefully it won't grow all weird like Billy's moustache."

Mrs. Sands lowered herself to Christian's height, kneeling as she did so. "Christian," she said sombrely, "Do you know what compassion is?" Christian knew that when Mrs. Sands got down to his level, she was telling him something important. He shook his head. "It's when you feel bad for somebody, but not in a bad way. It means you understand the bad things that have happened to them, and you understand their feelings."

"OK," said Christian, not sure where Mrs. Sands was going with what she was saying.

"Well, Billy was involved in a nasty accident a long time ago, before you were born, and it left his face scarred in a few places. One of them is just above his lip, meaning he can't grow a proper moustache, OK Christian nodded, his eyes facing the ground below him, as he knew that although she wasn't telling him off, she was teaching him a stern lesson. "So, we show compassion towards Billy, OK?"

"OK," he replied, still looking at the floor, "I'm sorry."

"Don't be sorry, Christian," she said as she rose to her feet, "because now that you know, you'll grow into a better person, alright? Big and strong like your dad."

"Have you seen him?" asked Christian, his saddened demeanour almost instantly vanishing at the mention of his father.

"He went up towards the lighthouse a little while ago," she replied, pointing to the path away from the square. Christian thanked her, and she ruffled his hair once again.

Making his way up towards the lighthouse, Christian noticed how the path seemed different from the others on the island. As it slowly curved to the right and up a small include, there was a selection of trees either side of him, each one no taller than he was. He couldn't remember the last time he'd been that way, but he definitely didn't remember the small trees being there. As the lighthouse came into view, the glass dome at the top revealing a stationary light that hadn't moved in years, Christian saw his father speaking to some of the other residents in the courtyard. Stepping closer, he could hear the deep tones of his father's voice, raspy like a long-time smoker, dictating something to the people around him. The closer Christian got, the more he could make out, and soon he could hear every word his father was saying.

He was stern, instructing the people around him where they'd be and at what times, but as Christian got closer, he suddenly stopped and turned his attention towards his child.

"Christian, good morning!" he said, his eyes wide as if he was both surprised and happy. He crouched slightly and threw his arms out wide, inviting Christian to come and hug him. As the two embraced, the people around him stayed quiet, almost as if they weren't there to witness the tender moment between father and son. "Christian, can you meet me by the fountain in about ten minutes? We've got something special to do today."

"But I was just there!" protested an angered Christian, but his father's raised finger told him everything he needed to know, and he stopped almost immediately. As Christian turned and began making his way back to the square, a voice came from behind him.

"So, what's happening then, Richie? Are we going for him tonight, or?" said the voice, before Christian heard a hard-slapping sound. He knew not to turn around, as his father had repeatedly told him that his business was not Christian's, and that he shouldn't interfere with things he didn't understand.

After waiting by the fountain for a short while, Christian's father came into view; his large beard and shoulder-length hair making him easy to spot in a crowd. Seeing his father's beard reminded Christian of the hairs he'd spotted that morning, but his father signalled for him to follow before he could mention them. Following closely behind, Christian noticed a gun of some type on his father's back, held on by a leather strap that hung over his shoulder. Christian asked what it was, but his father ignored him as he continued to make his way towards the forest, greeting everyone they passed. Christian's father was well-liked among the community, with many of the residents coming to him for help and advice when they needed it. Although he wasn't in charge and was still fairly new to the island, Christian often thought of his father as the unofficial leader, and he felt as though many of the residents thought the same.

As the two approached the end of the path, Christian could see only woodland ahead of them. He turned to his father, looking for either reassurance or instruction, and found the latter as his father crouched under the low-hanging branches and made his way into the forest. For a while, Christian struggled to keep up, his small legs not managing to reach the heights of his father's as he strode over fallen tree trunks and around muddy patches. Soon enough, the trees were behind them, and in front of Christian was a huge metal structure. Whatever it was looked brand-new, and like nothing he'd ever seen on the island before. As Christian stared upward at the structure, his head tilted all the way back, his father turned to him, pulling the weapon from his back around to the front.

"Christian," he said sternly, "if you get lost, or scared, or anything like that, you come here and you wait for me, OK? Tell me that you understand." Christian, whose heart was beginning to beat faster and faster, repeated his father's instruction, before questioning why they were there. "I'm going to teach you how to hunt, Christian. It's something that I hope you don't ever need to do, but it's important that you learn."

After a while of traipsing around in the woods, Christian's feet began to hurt. They'd only been out for an hour or so, but he was already getting bored. His father explained the importance of patience in hunting, but Christian didn't quite understand what he meant. He asked his father several times what they were hunting for but got no reply. After what must have been the sixth or seventh time, his father stopped and turned to his son as he had done outside of the metal structure.

"Christian, when you're hunting, you need to understand that it's either you or them. There's no in-between. If you become complacent and soft, you'll soon no longer be the hunter, but you'll become the hunted."

"But what are we hunting for? I mean, what's the reason?" asked Christian, raising his voice to match the volume of his father's.

"You'll soon learn, my boy. Maybe not today, but you will learn."
The two continued to tread lightly through the forest, careful not
to make any large sounds that would scare away the prey that
Christian had yet to see.

"What about compassion?" he asked, still not fully understanding
what it meant.

"Compassion?" came the reply from his father. "What about it?"

"Don't we have compassion for whatever we're hunting for?"

"Where did you learn that?" his father replied, continuing to look
ahead of him. Christian began to bite his nails, wondering if he
shouldn't have said anything. After his father asked for a second
time, Christian plucked up the courage to tell him that Mrs. Sands
had taught him about it. "Listen to me," his father said as he
turned around, the stench of his breath hanging in the air long
after he spoke, "compassion is for the weak. If you want to achieve
greatness in life, you have to be ruthless, doing what others can
only dream of. If you chose to live your life compassionately and
empathetically, you'll end up becoming a slave to somebody else
who had the will to do what needed to be done!" By now, his
father was almost shouting, the rasp of his voice echoing around
the trees that loomed over them. Christian wasn't entirely sure he
knew what his father meant, but he was sure that he didn't agree.

The two continued through the woods, stalking what felt like
nothing to Christian, his father keeping his rifle firmly gripped the
entire time. Occasionally he'd push his arm out towards Christian,
signalling for him to stop, but after a few seconds of listening, he'd
continue forward. Christian had always loved nature and being
outside, but since his father had brought him to the island, he
didn't have the chance to enjoy it as much as he used to. As he
studied the trees and fallen branches around them, searching for

insects, his father angrily beckoned him forward. Careful not to upset him, Christian followed his father's order immediately.

His father pointed ahead towards something that Christian couldn't see, but he nodded in approval anyway. His father then pointed to their left and right, where Christian could see several of the men his father had been speaking to also hiding amongst the trees. Whatever it was they were hunting for, Christian was the only one who couldn't see it, as the others were all pointing their rifles in the same direction as his father.

Before Christian could think too much about why they needed so many people to hunt one animal, his father had raised his rifle, the sights of the barrel lined up with his right eye. Christian knew this meant he had to be silent, but as he placed his hands on his ears to muffle the impending shot, he saw that the fellow hunters on his left and right had stood up and were now making their way presumably towards the target. Although his hands muffled the sound, he could hear that they were shouting, their rifles raised and pointed in front of them as they took brisk steps towards the unknown target. Soon, Christian's father joined them, his rifle pointed in the same direction. He began to shout too, louder than the others and more aggressively. Christian shuffled from side to side, hoping to get a better view of whatever the men were shouting at, but he couldn't see anything. He began to wonder what kind of animal you could hunt by shouting at it and waving your rifle around, but before long he was shocked to the core by the piercing sound of gunshots. He clamped his hands tighter to his ears as the shots repeated, over and over, each one feeling as though they were hitting him as well as their intended target.

After what felt like an age of shooting, the men lowered their rifles, the sound of the final shot still ringing around the forest and bouncing off the trees. Christian still didn't know what it was they'd been hunting, but he was sure that the dozens of shots from close range had ended the hunt. He could see the men standing around their target, looking down as if they'd discovered some kind of new species. They looked amazed and almost shocked that the several shots each of them had fired had actually killed it, even though Christian still couldn't see what it was that laid at their feet.

He began to creep forward, hoping to get a better look at the kill, but his father had already started towards Christian, signalling for his son to follow. His father's face now had specks of red dotted all over it, and as he wiped his sleeve across his face, the specks smudged, creating dark red lines from one side to the other. He wiped them again, and soon they'd disappeared. Christian checked over his shoulder for one last look, and he saw that the men were now pulling blue aprons over their heads and attaching surgical masks to their faces, making them almost completely unrecognisable. He saw the group wrap whatever it was they'd hunted in a large black cloth, before dragging it in the other direction out of view.

As Christian's father lead the way back to town, his attitude seemed different. For a man who was usually fairly reserved and kept his emotions to himself, he smiled excitedly almost the entire way, as if he was proud of himself. Christian hadn't seen his father this happy for a long time. Thinking back, the last time he'd seen him this elated was the day he'd brought the two of them to the island, which Christian had thought was strange even at the time. He often wondered why this had made him smile, considering his father had told him that they'd moved because Christian's mother didn't want him anymore.

The two approached the edge of the woods, and as the cobblestone pathway came into view, Christian's father crouched down next to him, holding him by the shoulders as he spoke softly.

"Christian, listen to me. Things are about to change here, but you have to trust me. Do you trust me?" He suddenly looked frightened, like the only thing that mattered in that moment was the trust of his son. Although he wasn't sure if he did, Christian nodded, his father sighing in relief as he did. "I need you to know, Christian, I am not a perfect person, but everything I do, I do for you, OK?"

"OK, dad," said Christian, tentatively, "but I didn't get to see what we hunted in the woods."

"Don't worry about that, Christian," his father said assuredly as he rose to his feet, "I'm going to drop you off with Mrs. Sands for a while, alright? Tonight, I need you to dress as nicely as you can and do your hair. We're going to have a special dinner, and I need you to look your best."

His father had been right. Throughout the rest of the day, Christian felt as if the adults had all been looking at him differently. Where previously they'd smiled at him and played with him, they now looked at him seriously, a coldness in their eyes. Christian wasn't sure what his father had done, but he didn't think he liked it, as he now felt intimidated by the adults, even with the well-liked Mrs. Sands by his side. She was the only one who hadn't looked at him differently and treated him the same as she had done before.

That afternoon she played chess with him, something Christian was sure that she purposely lost from time to time to make him feel like he was improving. She often denied Christian's request for the two of them to play football outside on the cobblestone, preferring for him to partake in something more educational, but today was different. After the two had finished a few games of chess, they headed outside to kick a ball around – something neither of them were very good at.

Before long, Mrs. Sands instructed Christian to collect his smartest clothes, telling him she'd help him look as smart as possible. Christian obliged, holding them high above his head as he ran back to her room, careful not to let them touch the ground. He'd picked up a smart shirt and trousers that the captain, an older man who Christian didn't see much, had brought to the island one day. He'd arrived with them along with some other items that he thought might be useful for the residents, but Christian's father had snapped up the small-sized clothing before the captain had even made it ashore. The clothes were still too big for Christian, and although Mrs. Sands tried her best to roll them up whilst still looking smart, it didn't work very well. She finished off the look by tying one of her husband's ties around Christian's neck, remarking how she had to tie it for her husband whenever he wore it. She stepped back, admiring Christian's outfit, holding a hand to her mouth to hide a large smile.

"You look so handsome, Christian! You're going to be the most handsome man in the room at dinner."

"I don't feel very handsome," he said, holding his arms up as the sleeves rolled down past his hands. Mrs. Sands pulled two silver armbands from the drawer and slipped them over Christian's wrists. She ruffled the shirt past the armbands, and soon enough the sleeves sat comfortably on Christian's wrists. Noticing the time, she hurried him to the door, brushing bits of fluff off his back as he made his way down the stairs. As the two reached the doorway, Mrs. Sands spun him round, checking him over one last time. Just as Christian was ready to make his way outside, Mrs. Sands leant forward and kissed him on the forehead as if he were her own. Christian, confused as to why the middle-aged lady had shown this sign of affection, didn't want to keep his father waiting. His shoes made a loud thudding sound with every step he took. As he looked over his shoulder to wave goodbye to his friend, he could see that she once again had a hand over her mouth, only this time, she was crying.

Christian made his way up towards the lighthouse, where his father had told him the big dinner was due to take place. As he made his way along the curved path once again, the tip of the lighthouse came into view. He began to wonder what it was like inside of a lighthouse, as the thin structure didn't leave much room for anything. He wondered if anyone had ever lived in a lighthouse, or if it was even possible. Seeing the small building at the base of the lighthouse, he assumed it wasn't. Whoever had been in charge of the lighthouse when it was still operational must have lived there, which disappointed Christian.

Soon enough, Christian stood in the open courtyard, and as he adjusted the armband that was holding up his sleeve, he could hear his father's voice calling out to him. He was dressed in a crushed velvet suit with a puffed tie and waistcoat – an outfit that Christian had never seen him wearing before. He was a far cry from the hunter Christian had seen this morning, now carrying himself with an air of authority, his shoulders back and his head held high. As Christian opened his arms to embrace his father, he ignored it, choosing to smarten his son's hair instead. He placed his hand at the top of Christian's back, and began pushing him forward, as if he wanted to present his son in some way. The two made their way towards the small building at the base of the lighthouse, which contained a bar-like area with many chairs and tables scattered around the room. Many of the seats were already filled by the residents of the island, most of which Christian recognised. At the far end of the room was the largest table, with two seats still vacant. Christian's father led them over to the two empty chairs, but it wasn't until Christian sat down that he noticed that everybody in the room was facing their way. They were all looking at him and his father, who had yet to take a seat, preferring instead to stand and face the residents, his hands together in front of him.

"Ladies and gentlemen, can I have your attention for a short time, please?" Christian's father addressed the crowd. As his voice bellowed out across the room, the residents fell silent, hanging on his every word. Christian knew that the residents often looked as father as a type of leader, but this was the first time he'd seen it for himself. "I have bad news to report. Earlier today, we found Stuart out in the woods. It seems that the island became a bit too much for him, as he was gone by the time we found him." As he bowed his head, some of the residents began to talk quietly amongst themselves. Christian wondered when this had happened and thought maybe his father had returned to the woods once he had taken him to Mrs. Sands. "Rest assured," he said as he swung his head upright, startling the people sat closest to him, "that I will not allow this to spoil our way of life here. The moment we discovered what had happened to Stuart, I decided to take action. As of tomorrow, I will be taking up the temporary position of mayor of Galkirk, until we can organise a proper election process."

The room hung on his every word, looking at him with wide eyes and closed mouths. "Tomorrow, we will have a memorial service for Stuart, and I hope everybody can make it. But for now," he said with a wicked smile on his face, "Mrs. Sands has kindly offered to cook for us all. We will eat, have fun, and celebrate the life of Stuart. As, without him, we wouldn't all be where we are today." He raised his glass, and soon the room followed his lead, raising their glasses high in the air. Christian looked up at his father, who was still gesturing towards the room, soaking up every drop of attention. He still didn't understand what was happening, but he could see that his father was having the time of his life.

After finishing his speech, Christian's father led the room outside to the courtyard, where Mrs. Sands had set up a stall, complete with a large grill and table. On the table sat empty bread buns next to a plate of grilled meat patties. Christian's father instructed everybody dig in, and before long, most of the residents were stood around the courtyard eating. His father made up two rolls, one for him, and one for Christian, but Christian held he burger in front of him, staring at it.

"What's wrong?" asked his father, but he didn't reply. He continued to look at the food in his hands, studying its every aspect.

"Is this what we hunted earlier? I'm not sure I can eat it." Looking disgruntled, his father took a knee so that he was once again eye-level with his son.

"Of course you can, Christian, it's good for you."

"But it was an animal in the woods," he said sadly, "I don't like that."

"Christian," said his father, "eating meat is natural. Animals do it, don't they? Just because things are a little different here, doesn't mean we should change who we are. Go ahead, try a bite, I know you'll like it."

Obeying his father's wish, Christian took a bite. To his surprise, it was good. Very good. He took another bite, followed by a few smaller bites, and soon the roll was half-gone.

"There you go!" said his father proudly as he stood upright. "I told you, fantastic!"

"Dad," managed Christian with a mouthful of food, "can I ask you something?" He gestured with one hand for his father to get closer, and as he turned his ear towards his son, Christian continued, whispering quietly. "When did you find Stuart? Was it after we went hunting?"

Without answering, his father stood up, the same wicked smile upon his face. He ruffled his son's hair playfully, before taking the food from him and taking a bite for himself, which he seemed to enjoy significantly.

The next morning, Christian woke to the sound of his father rummaging through their drawers. Christian rubbed his eyes as he sat upright, wondering what the time was. As the room came into focus, he could see that there were clothes strewn everywhere – which was uncommon, considering how neat and tidy his dad usually was. Stood by the mirror was his father, frantically trying on different clothing whilst checking how his reflection looked. As he posed with a waistcoat held up to his chest, Christian could see in the reflection that his father had not only shaved off his beard but had also seemingly cut his hair to a much shorter length. He looked almost nothing like his previous self, and for a brief second, Christian wondered if he was actually dreaming. His father was humming joyfully, like he'd just received the best of news.

As his father turned to pick up a piece of clothing on the floor, he finally noticed that Christian was awake. His eyes widened, as if he'd forgotten all about his offspring that shared a room with him. He kissed him gently on the forehead, just how Mrs. Sands had done the day before, and offered to get his son some food. Christian declined, feeling like he was still full from last night's food, and checked the small clock on the bedside table. It was early, earlier than they would usually wake up, and a quick check out of the small window revealed that it was still dark outside. It was raining heavily, filling the empty fountain of the square. As Christian turned back towards his father, he saw that he was still deciding what to wear.

"What are we doing, dad? Why are we up so early?" Christian rubbed his eyes, as his vision had begun to blur again.

"We're doing our duty." His father spoke proudly as he continued to look at himself in the mirror. "We're doing our duty", he repeated, as if he were assuring himself of his own words.

"But what does that mean?"

"You know how Stuart welcomed us when we first arrived?" snapped his father as he began picking the clothes up off of the floor and stuffing them into the drawers. "Well, now that Stuart is gone, I've got to do that. And seeing as you're awake, you can come with me. It's a father and son, like you and me, and it'd be nice for him to make friends with someone around his own age."

After Christian had dressed himself, his father wrapped him in one of his coats before the two set off through the pouring rain towards the docks. Luckily, they didn't have to wait long. Within a few minutes, the dim lamp onboard the boat had become visible through the fog. As the boat got closer, Christian's father began to wave his arm in a large arch, as if greeting to a friend in the distance. The captain began to prepare the boat for docking, and soon the two new residents stepped off the boat – a tall man, and presumably his son, who was almost just as tall. If the son was in fact around Christian's age, he certainly didn't look it.

"Christian," asked his father, looking at the new arrivals, "how did you enjoy last night's dinner?"

"It was nice," he replied, looking up at the confident man that was his father, "why?" Although he didn't look down at his son, Christian could see that his father had a wild look in his eye, like a predator stalking its prey.

"Well, we're going to have it again tonight, my boy. Aren't you lucky?"

Chapter 13:
Ends.

Harold saw Sarah standing over him, the look on her face suggesting she was disappointed but not surprised. Harold could feel himself shaking, but he wasn't sure if it was the cold, the adrenaline, the fear, or a mixture of all three. Sarah crouched down beside him, placing her hand on the top of his head.

"Harold," she said softly, "I did what you asked, but I'm not sure how this is going to go. The captain leaves tomorrow, and I'm going to try and convince him to take me."

Harold, now somewhat calm, tried to sit up. His chest hurt, but he wasn't sure why. He still felt dizzy but could concentrate enough to know that Sarah was the last person he could trust.

"I can't go," said Harold sombrely, realising his reality, "If I try to get on the boat, someone will see me. After all that, everybody here knows who I am. Someone will spot me, and they'll stop us."

"We can find a way," said Sarah, a glimmer of hope in her eye. Harold shook his head, knowing that he would now never leave the island.

"You go," he said, "I know that this place isn't what we thought, and so do you. If you can make it off the island, you can tell people back home and we can still win."

Knowing he was right; Sarah bowed her head. "What will you do?" she said softly, but Harold ignored her. He turned away from her, closing his eyes and pulling the sheets up to his neck. Before he could drift off, he felt the sheets lift for a second, and as he looked over his shoulder, he saw Sarah settle down next to him. Before he could say anything, she'd pulled the sheets up over the both of them and placed her arm around his chest, holding him close.

The next morning Harold woke with a jolt, briefly forgetting where he was. As he began to comprehend what had happened the night before, he turned over, expecting to see Sarah. He was alone, and he wondered if his mind had played tricks on him once again. He thought about the events of the past few days and wondered how much of his memory he could trust. He knew what he'd seen, but the people around him had either seen different, or apparently changed their opinions. He felt as if he was losing his mind. Even Manu, someone he thought he could trust, had seemingly turned against him.

Deciding not to dwell too much on his mental state, Harold rose to his feet and stretched, feeling a bone in his spine click. He slapped his face to wake himself up and made his way out of the shed. Although he wasn't sure what was going on with the residents and his friends, he knew one thing –Christian had to be stopped. Feeling the rage and anger build up inside him, he began making his way towards the square.

Passing the large factory, Harold began to run through the possibilities of what had happened to Yvette, presuming she'd managed to get inside somehow. The tall structure loomed over Harold, the large windows and metal panels shining in the sun. The trees surrounding it swayed side to side as the wind blew through them, and kicking through the fallen leaves and branches, Harold continued on down the path past the trees and into the square.

He felt his confidence building. His shoulders were dropping with each step and his head was firmly fixed on what was in front of him. He could tell that his eyes were wide, but he began to feel as though he wasn't in control. He hadn't even noticed that he had left the forest and now walked along the stone path outside of his friend's shop. As the fountain came into view, Harold began to spot the residents pointing at him and whispering to people around them. He kept his eyes fixated on the fountain. He was on a mission, and nothing would stop him. Some of the residents tried to approach him with arms extended, a caring look in their eye, but he brushed them off as he paced towards the centre of the square. As he reached the fountain, he stopped suddenly, looking over his left and right shoulder at the group that had now formed around him. He breathed steadily, keeping his composure on the outside whilst the anger built up inside. Unlike yesterday, Harold felt as though he could see clearly now, and that all eyes were well and truly on him. He took a deep breath before releasing an almost primal scream, hoping to attract the last few residents that weren't looking at him yet. With everybody's attention and his head tipped downwards, he looked up at the people around him, his nostrils flaring and his breathing heavy like a predator searching for its prey.

"Christian!" he roared, "Get out here now, you monster!". Soon enough, Christian emerged from the crowd. He nonchalantly made his way past Charlie and Mrs. Sands, approaching Harold. When he got close, he stopped, his palms open and facing Harold, as if to show he was unarmed. He shrugged and then smiled, his casual approach only angering Harold further.

"You know I'm right," screamed Harold, his voice squeaking and breaking as he did, "now admit it! In front of all these people. Tell them I'm right. Tell them you're making us eat the residents who disappear. Tell them now!"

Christian made his way closer to Harold, his palms still raised. Whilst Harold could feel himself shaking with rage again, but Christian remained calm and collected as he came touching distance of Harold.

"Harold, I told you before, you're sick. You need help. You've needed help all along, but instead, you came here. I should have said no when you applied for residency here." He took a step closer to Harold, looking straight into his eyes. "For that, Harold, I'm sorry." Harold pushed him back, angered at his attempt to play the victim.

"Don't fucking patronise me, you psychopath! I know your secret, and now so does everybody else. Admit it and face the consequences."

Undeterred by Harold's aggression, Christian rolled up his sleeves up and cleared his throat.

"Citizens of Galkirk, I can only apologise for bringing Harold into our community," Christian proclaimed loudly to the audience surrounding them. "This man is clearly very unwell and needs professional help. But rest assured, I will take the necessary steps to ensure he gets help and continue to provide safety and security for you all."

Harold's rage boiled over, and without thinking he tackled Christian to the floor. As their bodies hit the ground, the crowd let out a collective gasp, and soon the two were engaged in physical combat. It wasn't until now that Harold realised exactly how much physically fitter than him Christian was, but he hoped that his blind rage would help him succeed. The two tussled on the floor for some time, until Christian kicked him away and stood up, lowering his fists.

"I won't fight you if I don't have to, Harold. But these people depend on me, and if you threaten us or our way of life, I will."

"I don't pose a threat to them or their way of life," replied Harold, wiping the blood from his lip as he stood to face Christian once again, "just you."

Harold threw a fist towards his opponent, which Christian dodged, before coming back with a fist of his own. He caught Harold right below the eye, rocking him badly. His eye had just begun to heal, but the fresh hit caused it to swell up again almost instantly.

Harold, still shocked from the punch, threw his other arm out towards Christian, hitting him squarely between the eyes. Surprisingly, Christian took the punch well, staggering backward but staying on his feet. The two exchanged several blows, each of them dealing some damage from time to time. After receiving several consecutive hits to the face, Harold tried to grapple with Christian, aiming his thumbs for Christian's eyes as he'd done to Maria's lover some time ago, but Christian was wise to it. He shrugged Harold off and returned an elbow that struck Harold on the side of his head. Staggered, Harold felt a crushing blow to his shin where Christian had kicked out at him, and as he fell to a knee, Christian kicked him in the face, dropping Harold to his back.

As Christian climbed on top of a broken and beaten Harold, he placed his hands around his neck. Squeezing firmly, he began to cut off Harold's airways, choking him. Harold tried to remove his foe's hands from his neck, but his grip tightened as he lowered his mouth towards Harold's ear.

"I found your little friend, Sarah. She's not going anywhere. Your plan has failed, and you have failed" he whispered, careful not to let the audience hear him. Harold's face began to turn blue as his fingers clawed at Christian's hands. "You've lost, my friend."

Harold's hands began to go limp, and his eyes started to roll towards the back of his head. "Life is- chess," he managed as Christian pressed down even harder on his neck. With his last breath, he barely mustered a final word. "Checkmate," he grunted, before his arms flopped to the floor and his head tilted back.

Christian, still grinding his teeth together, pushed from Harold's neck to help himself up. Harold's body laid still at his feet as he looked around him. The audience were in shock at what they'd seen, yet nobody wanted to speak out of turn, fearful of what they'd just witnessed. In an attempt to regain their trust, Christian spoke once again.

"Ladies and gentlemen, I am beyond sorry for what you all just had to witness. This man had previous troubles with his mental health, and I assumed it was something that we here at Galkirk could help him come to terms with. I was wrong." Christian spun around to face the audience behind him, before continuing to speak. "This is no excuse for violence, but you all saw what happened. He attacked me, but more importantly, he attacked our way of life and our attempt to start again. That is something I will not tolerate. So, if any of you have any objections to the way we do things here, please step forward. Know that I will not take to violence as Harold did, but rather I will speak to you, man to man, to resolve any issues you may have."

His voice echoed against the surrounding buildings, and as he looked around at the audience, they just stood there, quietly. Manu, Franziska, Charlie, neither they or anyone else stepped forward. "Very well," he continued, "then I ask that Doctor Halter help with the remains of our friend here and that the rest of you take the day off. Return to your homes, enjoy time with friends, do as you wish." Hanging on his every word, the crowd stayed quiet. As Doctor Halter carried Harold's body off down the cobblestone path, the crowd dispersed, leaving Christian alone in the centre of the square, bruised and bloodied, but still standing.

Later that evening, Christian showered and changed his clothes. His face looked a little worse for wear, and his lip had begun to swell, but for the most part, he was fine. After downing a drink from the bar in his sitting area, he made his way outside into the drizzling rain. He let the cool rain wash over his face for a while, as it soothed the aches and pains from the earlier confrontation. Dropping his head down after a few minutes, he made his way over to one of the buildings of the complex and placed his hands on the door. As he went to unlock the padlock, he looked over to the left at the building directly next to him – the one that Harold had opened at the party. He let out a sigh of relief and opened the door, revealing his father strapped into the chair in the centre of the dark room. Christian grabbed some meat from the fridge in the corner and began to feed his father, placing small clumps of raw meat in his mouth and rubbing the wrinkled skin of his throat.

"I killed Harold today, dad," he said sadly whilst continuing to feed his father, "but I didn't hesitate. I mean, the guy was a fucking loony, but he got close." Christian's father, who showed no signs of life other than the soft breathing, took no notice of his son. He simply swallowed when Christian rubbed his throat, grunting every so often.

As Christian held the last two pieces of meat, he fed one to his father, holding the second in the palm of his hand. He studied it, rolling it around as the juices spilled out and dropped to the floor. "I haven't tried it since I was a boy," he said to himself, his eyes fixed firmly on his hand and the meat that rolled around on it. He parted his lips, slowly placed the lump of meat on his tongue, and began to chew. The blood spurted out inside his mouth, the cold liquid making him squint and wince. It was stringy and tough, but after a few chews he'd mashed it down, and he swallowed the piece of meat. It wasn't unpleasant, but it had been a while for Christian, who was unsure if he enjoyed it or not. He placed the oxygen mask back over his father's mouth, kissed him on the forehead, and locked up the room.

As the sun began to set, Christian was sitting atop the remains of the lighthouse, looking out towards the sea. He could see a big part of the island from his elevated position. To one side he could see the forest and the tip of the factory as the last remaining sunlight bounced off of the roof, then the buildings of the square, and finally the docks, where the captain was preparing to disembark. He sat with his legs crossed, and soon he heard someone making their way up to his position. Looking down at the ladder he'd placed to reach the top of the lighthouse, he could see that Manu was climbing the makeshift ladder to him. Christian patted a space next to him, and Manu took a seat, crossing his legs also.

"It's been a funny few weeks, hasn't it?" said the Italian, looking out towards the docks. He untied his signature buns, letting his hair drop down his back. Christian looked over, jealous of Manu's locks, smiling playfully.

"You could say that, I suppose."

"Still, it's lucky that he believed you about Charlie and the store, eh? I'm not quite sure how that worked so well."

"He was extremely unstable," said Christian, confidently, "and as soon as he started doubting himself, it became easy. They start to think erratically. I mean, ask yourself this; he took Jerry's diary, right? So how could he have ever questioned that it *was* his shop?"

"I'm not sure," sighed Manu, "still, I'm glad it's all over."

"Oh no, my friend. We're near the finishing line, but we're not done yet. I've got one or two more loose ends to sort, my friend, and then we're back to normal."

"Like what?" asked Manu.

"It's nothing to worry about, my friend. All I will say is this: I may need you to return to the mainland for short while. Can I trust you with that?"

Manu nodded, and the two looked out at the boat sailing away from the docks and into the distance. As it disappeared from view, Christian's stomach began to growl.

"Did Doctor Halter sort out the body?" he asked, trying to spot the boat in the distance. Manu nodded again.

"He took it to the factory. He'll be ready by tonight."

"Good," replied Christian, "and Sarah? What did he do with her?"

"I think he put her in with the dead pigs, why?"

"I'm feeling a bit peckish," said Christian, rubbing his stomach as it growled once again.

Epilogue.

"Cheese and pickle, or ham and mustard?" called Maria to the hallway, but there was no response. She tried again, louder and sterner, but heard nothing. "Cheese, pickle, ham, *and* mustard it is then," she said sarcastically, "that's what you get for paying more attention to model trains than you do to your wife."

As she sliced the sandwich in half, Maria thought she heard something being stuffed through the letterbox, and clap of the flap confirmed it. She strolled through the large hallway of her house, passing the pictures of the two of them together that she'd had printed some years ago. As she saw the pile of letters that had come through the door, she stopped. Glancing over her shoulder to the last photo on the wall, she turned and gave it her full attention. It showed the two of them on their wedding day, and although it wasn't of the greatest quality, it was one of her favourites. She felt her stomach as she noticed how thin she was in the picture, and she brushed the back of her hand on the picture of his face, seeing how happy he had been that day. He stood proudly in the suit his dad had worn on his wedding day, and behind them stood their friends and family who'd joined them in the celebrations. Although they'd been throwing confetti, the photograph didn't capture most of it, so instead it looked like the crowd were gesturing strangely towards the two newlyweds.

Letting out a happy sigh, Maria turned towards the door and collected the pile of post that had accumulated on the doormat. Most of it was the usual bills and flyers for local businesses, but one specific envelope captured her interest. It was handwritten and addressed to her but had no address or postage stamp on it. Wondering how it had reached her, she assumed a neighbour had put it through her door, and as she inspected the envelope, she saw it was worse for wear, looking as though it had been mistreated on its way to her.

"Has my package arrived?" came a voice from the other room. "It won't be big, it's just a new conductor and some bushes for the hillside."

"Sorry love, it's not here yet. Just bills and stuff." Replied Maria. As she stood inspecting the envelope further, Thomas made his way into the hallway, struggling to push the wheels of his wheelchair along the thick carpet below. Thomas, who had finally gotten used to using his wheelchair, reached down to scratch at his leg. However, he was met by the feeling of cold metal, and as he looked down, he felt a crushing sadness. He was experiencing phantom pain, and as he looked at the metal replacements he'd been fitted with some weeks ago, he tried to take his mind off things.

"We've got to get rid of this," he said, gesturing at the carpet, "you always say how it's full of the cat's hair anyway. Why don't we upgrade to something nice like tile or wood?"

"You leave Coco alone." Maria hadn't taken her eyes off of the envelope, staring at the handwriting on the front. "Besides, where are we going to get the money for a front room full of wooden flooring? You keep spending all of our money on your bloody trains." Despite the fact that what she was saying was mean-spirited, she said it in a loving and joking way. As she began to let out fake laughter, she stopped suddenly, realising she recognised the handwriting on the front of the envelope.

"I'm not having a go, you know I love her. But I just think it'd be better for her *and* me if we got something nicer and-" he paused, noticing his wife's concerned look. "What's that?"

"I think it's from that stalker I had years ago, I recognise the writing from the creepy love letters he used to send me."

Thomas frowned, annoyed at Maria's choice of wording. "Stalker? The stalker? You mean mentally unstable freak who thought he was married to you and did this to me?" He waved his hands over his legs. "I'm calling the police." He tried to turn his wheelchair, but the thick carpet made it hard for him to make any tight manoeuvres.

"No, wait!" she cried, making Thomas jump. "On the news, they said he went missing a while ago. Maybe we should read it? It might explain where he went?"

"Why do you care, Maria? He should have been put in prison for all the stalking and weird things he used to do, let alone for fucking attacking me! I say we burn it and let him fade into obscurity, wherever he is."

Ignoring him, she opened it up and skipped straight to the bottom to confirm her suspicions – it was from Harold. Before she could return to the top to read the letter through, a knock came from behind the front door. Peering through the letterbox, Maria could see that on the other side was a man in loose-fitted clothing, smoking a cigarette. His hair was tied up into two tight buns that sat on top of his head, and under his eyes sat two dark bags as if he'd not slept in days.

"Hello, Maria," said the man through the letterbox, "you don't know me, but I think a letter has been wrongly delivered to you. My wife wrote the wrong name on the front, so I posted it through just now, then realised she told me she'd put the wrong name on the front. Can I have it back?"

Suspicious of the man behind the door, Maria turned to look at her husband, but he shrugged, before continuing to try and turn his wheelchair on the carpet.

"Who are you?" she asked, cautiously placing a hand on the door handle.

"My name is, um," He paused briefly, "Christian. My name is Christian. If you can simply open the door, I'll explain the mix-up and get it all sorted out. I'll be out of your way before you know it."

Lightning Source UK Ltd.
Milton Keynes UK
UKHW022000310321
381341UK00003B/335